DESCENT INTO DARKNESS

Descent
Into
Darkness

JAY TROY SEATE

Sense of Wonder Press
JAMES A. ROCK & COMPANY, PUBLISHERS
ROCKVILLE • MARYLAND

Descent into Darkness by Jay Troy Seate

SENSE OF WONDER PRESS
is an imprint of JAMES A. ROCK & CO., PUBLISHERS

Descent into Darkness copyright ©2007 by Jay Troy Seate

Special contents of this edition copyright ©2007
by James A. Rock & Co., Publishers

All applicable copyrights and other rights reserved worldwide. No part of this publication may be reproduced, in any form or by any means, for any purpose, except as provided by the U.S. Copyright Law, without the express, written permission of the publisher.

This book is a work of fiction. While some names, places, and events, are historically correct they are used fictitiously to develop the storyline and should not be considered historically accurate. Any resemblance of the characters in this book to actual persons, living or dead, is coincidental and beyond the intent of either the author or the publisher.

Address comments and inquiries to:
SENSE OF WONDER PRESS
James A. Rock & Company, Publishers
9710 Traville Gateway Drive, #305
Rockville, MD 20850

E-mail:
jrock@rockpublishing.com   lrock@rockpublishing.com
Internet URL: www.rockpublishing.com

ISBN: 978-1-59663-556-2
1-59663-556-8

Library of Congress Control Number: 2007929270

Printed in the United States of America

First Edition: 2007

Contents

Mr. Herndon's Blood 1

Dirty Bird 6

Where The Gods Feast 13

Laura's Dream 26

Shadow Boy 33

A Tale For The Trail 38

Houseguest 44

The Man On The Bathroom Floor 53

My Pretty Painted Pony 57

Dancing With A Blind Girl 65

Detained 73

Cottage For Sale 80

Descent Into Darkness 89

Acknowledgments

A special thanks to Sandra Kregar who co-authored *My Pretty Painted Pony* and to her mother, Jo, for introducing me to Mr. Herndon.

Foreword

As with everyone who sits in front of a monitor or a blank piece of paper attempting to create, the first word begins an adventure of the mind that you are compelled to experience for yourself. The sharing comes later. If you're brave, you want to expose both the dark corners and the moments of bright revelation, pulling along people you don't even know and hoping they find your adventures frightening or joyous or whimsical.

Stephen King once suggested that in the literary world, his writing was the equivalent of a Big Mac™ and fries. If that is so, my efforts could be the equivalent of a Good Times Drive-Thru.™ But I don't care. I like what I like, especially if the trip through the drive-thru is brief.

I've compiled twelve short stories of fear and the unknown based on both the real and unreal to accompany my paranormal mystery, *Descent into Darkness*. The tales might be humorous or erotic depending on my characters, who are often unreceptive to logic or reason, the murky rascals. I offer a few brief comments on each tale to guide you through safely. I hope you find your fun house, fast-food stop entertaining.

J. Troy Seate

When a neighbor told me what she used to give her rose bushes a little extra oomph, I knew this story had to be written.

Mr. Herndon's Blood

Mr. Herndon arrived at four o'clock on the dot.

"Good afternoon, my two wild, beautiful flowers," he said jovially.

Not a surprising moniker considering my name is Rose and my co-worker is named Iris. It was my week to draw blood from the bulging-eyed, corpulent Mr. Herndon. He suffered from an uncommon condition know as polycythemia, meaning too many red blood cells. The unfortunate fellow looked a fright at each appointment. His egg-yolk corneas were no less appealing than the rest of his face, swelled to the size of a beach ball, his extremities, bloated into spoiled, hairy sausages.

We dutifully phlebotomized Mr. Herndon for months and, to the man's credit, he maintained a sense of humor, even though his blood pressure was higher than his bank balance and his words tended to be luridly off-color. Iris and I teased one another about which of us Mr. Herndon had the biggest crush on, but our sarcasm and innocent barbs stopped abruptly when he missed an appointment.

1

Mr. Herndon had died from a clot in his brain the day after his last bloodletting. The rotund, little man had been particularly flirty and raucous that day, one final attempt to impress us with his randy wit.

The news came just as Iris was lecturing me about the proper care of my flowering plants and my apparent lack of a green thumb. "You know what you need for your rosebush?" Iris had asked. "A few red blood cells. I put some congealed stuff around my roots and everything perked right up."

We had no shortage of blood at the clinic, so at the end of the day, I pilfered a plastic bag from the freezer. "Come with me, Mr. Herndon," I wistfully said. "Your blood won't be missed and you can help my garden grow, you poor man."

That very evening, I juiced my scrawny, blighted rosebush with Mr. Herndon's blood. I had heard of people wrapping placentas around their rosebushes. The next best thing to having a dead body underneath my garden, I mused, but blood was gruesome enough. I took care to dig a trench around the bush's trunk and cover it with topsoil, hoping the neighborhood felines wouldn't be attracted to the scent. The pint soaked in quickly.

As you have probably guessed, my rosebush turned from an ugly duckling to a healthy swan with shiny green leaves and velvety red buds. I actually gasped with each sight of them. They blossomed quicker than I thought possible into dark, crimson beauties. To be honest, they frightened me. Mr. Herndon's blood had certainly done the trick, but my rosebush revival had been too quick, too unnatural.

An interloper did attempt to plunder the fresh soil, however. I heard what sounded like a catfight. Upon investigation, I found cat fur twisted around a thorn and droplets of blood leading from the bush to my cedar fence. "You're supposed to be poised and pretty—not a fighter," I told the rosebush. If not for a breeze murmuring gently amongst the floral inhabitants of my backyard,

I would have sworn the plant sighed in response. Don't encourage this bizarre rehabilitation, I thought, then felt foolish about my misgivings.

One evening, I stood at my kitchen window doing dishes as the setting sun cast its dying rays over the leaves and petals of my healthiest garden plant. The leaves had increased dramatically in size since I'd last taken notice. They didn't look like most rosebush leaves. They looked more like the spreading appendages of maple leaves. More like ...

Hands with fingers.

As I watched, a leaf trembled then closed in on itself, opened and closed again, beckoning to me. I turned from the window stringing sudsy water across the counter and onto the floor. My breathing halted long enough for a train to pass. I had to remind myself to use my lungs.

This wouldn't do. Hr. Herndon's rosebush was more than frightening. It was playing tricks with my psyche. So beautiful, much more so than its benefactor, rest his soul, yet so forbidden, so ... sickeningly malevolent. Still, I couldn't bring myself to destroy this creation, but I could relocate it.

I moved it from its sunny spot in my backyard to a dark, dank place on the north side of my home's foundation. Perhaps there, virtually without life-giving sunlight, it would wither and die. It's destiny was no longer in my hands but in Mother Nature's.

A week passed. In its new location, Mr. Herndon's rosebush had shown no signs of withering. Instead it became a climber and leaned its thorny stalks topped by its perfect buds against the house. When stirred by the slightest breeze, its thorns scratched against the siding.

It's trying to get in, I often worried, as I tossed and turned in bed and thought of how Mr. Herndon used to leer at me with his sad, bulbous features that surrounded his bulging eyes. This had to stop, beautiful roses or not.

Following a sleepless night, I approached the rosebush with my trusty garden hoe and marveled again at the speed with which the stalks were climbing, topped by the furry flowers, getting nearer my bedroom window.

A large, gray tomcat as fascinated as I, and apparently still drawn to the plant's scent, lay near the rosebush, flirting with danger. His tail whipped from side to side as if hypnotized by a hole full of mice.

"Get " I hissed. Tom raised his hackles and lay his ears back but refused to retreat. "Pssst," I added. He looked at me with disgust, then turned tail and ran. Now, just the two of us, Mr. Herndon's rosebush and me. I came closer to the plush roses … too close not to see.

Walk away, my mind pleaded with my feet. *Walk away once and for all*, but my body wouldn't obey. Curiosity of a cat, you might say. Even as my mind fought to reject the plant's latest behavior, my eyes saw.

At its base, the earth had softened and turned dark. Not from water. I hadn't watered since I'd carelessly replanted. The soil was too dark for water.

Blood

Its root pulsated like a heartbeat. The topmost rose had fully blossomed. It was that flower that almost took away my rational world. Its blood red petals lay open invitingly as I looked closely. My eyes blinked rapidly and grew hot. My saliva turned to sand. I was unable to speak. My hands were welded to the handle of my garden hoe.

I couldn't look away from the bloom's revelation. Mr. Herndon's features rested within its folds. His gaping mouth lay between two rows of petals. Two raised, black spots on an otherwise unblemished petal were his bulging eyes.

I gaped, transfixed and again willed my body to respond. I knew I had to act quickly or forever be lost, pulled into Mr.

Herndon's thorny caress. I raised the hoe and swung with all my strength. The blade caught the rose's stem, forcing it to the ground. The stem didn't break. A petal fell away ... *an ear.*

The plant's frenzied pulse raced through the stems to the other blossoms as they bent toward me. I placed my foot on Mr. Herndon's rose and raised my hoe again. A thorn somehow found my ankle and ripped the skin, but I was undaunted. Down came my blade a second time and severed the rose as I pitilessly ground the flower beneath my heel.

An internal scream exploded in my skull as the bush sprang back to its upright position, spraying a thin line of crimson up my pant leg. The surviving uppermost rose seemed to unfold to its maximum circumference, replacing its fallen comrade. I stepped back, afraid to take my eyes from the plant as it replenished itself.

I thought of ways to destroy Mr. Herndon's rosebush but nothing short of pulling it from the earth by its roots would suffice. Perhaps, even then, the saturated ground would seed another unholy flora in its dark womb to pursue me.

***

Yesterday, I did what I pray will let me sleep again. I gave a pint of blood at the clinic and brought it home. I dug a new hole along the foundation of my house. I buried a new plant and poured my blood around its roots, careful to keep it between Mr. Herndon and myself, while apologizing for my previous actions.

Will my new rosebush flourish ... and satisfy its companion? I can only hope the blood from one of Mr. Herndon's "wild, beautiful flowers" might settle him down. But for now, I won't return to that side of the house and I've nailed plywood over my bedroom window.

On the lighter side, no collection would be complete without giving someone the bird. And, by the way, this story is based on a true event in the life of your humble servant.

Dirty Bird

Although I'd never kept a bird as a pet, I had nothing against them. I cursed whenever one dive-bombed my windshield but other than that, we respected each other's place in the universe ... until the nasty, dirty bird came into my life.

He did not start out as nasty, just as a nuisance, sitting on an evergreen peering in through a window. Then, he started his infernal fluttering against the windowpanes. From one room to another, he'd fly against the glass obstructions, leaving dirty claw-foot doodles behind.

I tried to figure out his problem. Had he been sleeping on the job as his flock migrated south? Was he domesticated and searching for a new home? Maybe he was the spirit of a deceased friend or relative trying to communicate.

In the beginning, he was non-descript, larger than a sparrow but smaller than the magpies that often bashed about, stealing nuts put out for squirrels. Not being a bird aficionado, I hadn't a clue as to what type of bird he might be. The widow next door said he might be some variety of woodpecker. If so, he was out of luck against my vinyl siding.

I often sauntered outdoors and talked to the bird while neighbors peered out of their windows convinced I was nuttier than they had previously thought. He would fly safely to a tree limb where he swiveled his gray, little head and mocked me with his cold black eyes.

In time, he turned his attention to my trusty transportation, assaulting it with piles of bird dung. He perched on my side-view mirrors and pooped piles of black and green goo mixed with birdseed. I tried to short-circuit these shit-fits by garaging my vehicle, but he swooped right in and did his thing. He was much too fast for the electric garage door or my attempts to trap him with a sheet. In ten seconds flat, he could deliver a load of bird crap on both mirrors and leave another mother load on my door handle.

There was no refuge.

I decided I had been the birdbrain. Shiny objects attract him. There wasn't much I could do about the reflective windows on my car or house, but I could cover my car mirrors with white plastic bags before the bird from Hell had a chance to strike. If I removed shiny surfaces and the food supply I kept out for sensible birds, surely he would move on.

He was not at all happy with my ploy. When I opened my garage to go out, he would flutter around the windows and crap on my windshield even as I pulled away. I tried unsuccessfully to deter him with my squirting wiper fluid. *That dirty little shit-bird*, I thought. What was it going to take? I won't let him in and I've taken away his shiny perches. Next he'll be dive-bombing me when I go for the morning paper.

I considered hiring a fifteen-year-old kid with a BB-gun to take him out, but old lady Wallace next door would never have forgiven me, her being a naturist and all. She was a resourceful old gal though. She watched as I frantically waved my hands trying to intimidate my feathered friend. Knowing the bird was in as much distress as I, she produced a non-harmful live trap to help end my misery.

I once again offered my vehicle up as bait. The plastic bags came off and I placed the metal cage with birdseed leading inside on my car's roof. This act was followed by two days of an unrelenting shit storm directed at my once proud automobile. Of course, my bird couldn't have cared less about the metal grate holding the seeds. In fact he perched and dropped bird-turds on the trap, chirping happily.

I sweetened the deal with a sliver of peanut-buttered bread and moved the trap to the top of my car's trunk. This action succeeded in trapping a freaked-out squirrel that managed to topple his prison and drag it down the drive a distance.

It was then I let my fingers do the walking over the phone book. I called every possibility, from animal control to wildlife organizations. They all said the same thing. They didn't get involved with the capture or removal of wildlife.

This dirty bird had bested me and I was desperate. My hands seemed permanently wrinkled from washing shit off my car. By now, I was certain I could have picked him out of a whole flock. My thoughts once again turned to the neighborhood gunslinger but then, miracle of miracles, I heard the trap slam shut in my garage.

No unsuspecting, wayward squirrel or chipmunk this time, no sirreeee. It was my gray tormentor trapped within. His feathers were puffed out, making him almost too large for his cell. While he batted around, I acted quickly. Spreading newspaper over my backseat, I placed the cage and prisoner inside, climbed in the car and headed for an open space a good eight miles from my house.

While in route, I consoled my nemesis. "I'm glad our relationship is ending in a mutually agreeable way," I said to him. "I'm the kind of guy who is willing to relocate you rather than break your little neck."

I parked and carried the cage fifty yards to a place with tall weeds, trees and a virtual bird-cornucopia of wild seeds, worms and who-knows-what. I opened the trapdoor and said, "So long."

His cold black eyes scrutinized me, I imagined. I coaxed him out with a gentle shove of a stick. He flew a short distance, perched on a limb and eyeballed me further.

"I'm not going to feel guilty, you little so and so. Find a girlfriend and crap all you want out here.

I departed, anxious to return the trap to one-eyed Mrs. Wallace.

At this point, I know you are way ahead of me. No sooner had I put my digit on Mrs. Wallace's doorbell than I heard a familiar trill. "No. Impossible." I walked to my house and there sat my dirty bird on a dead tree branch dropping a fresh load in my driveway.

Could there have been more than one, I pondered? Unlikely. More unlikely than the hard fact that he had found his way back by following the car or he possessed that innate ability birds obviously have. They fly thousands of miles from season to season. Why not eight?

I entered my refuge, dulled with a sense of defeat, proceeded to the bar and mixed myself a strong, nasty one. In moments, I heard my old companion softly fluttering against my windowpane. Walking to the window, I watched as he lit on a bush then ran into the window again, wings splayed and claws seeking traction, then fly to the bush again. Lifting my glass I said, "Here's to you, my crazy-ass feathered friend. I guess you win … for now."

I thought the winged beast was my only problem until my doorbell rang one evening around five. On my front porch stood a man named Harvey Deets. He was soused to the gills. Reluctantly I opened the door. My eyes watered from the aroma of the brew that clung to him like an overcoat.

"What is it?" I asked, fearful that I knew exactly what Harvey was here for. I had contracted Deets to repair the roof over my front porch last fall. He promised a two-week job. Over the next two months, I let him bilk me out of most of the money with cheap talk about one hardship or another. He had shown up a few times accomplishing little before the weather turned cold. Finally fed up, I called his answering machine and told him not to bother coming back. In a word, he was fired.

I figured he would be delighted considering he had been paid for most of the project and done next to no repair. But now, here he stood on my porch, liquored up and in a surly mood, demanding the balance.

I told him not only "No" but, "Hell no."

After we traded a few insults, I noticed the two goons loitering around his truck. By this time, Harvey and I were standing in the yard pointing up to what had or had not been done, depending on who was talking.

When I ordered him off my property, he waved to his *compadres*. They tromped through lava rock toward us looking more pissed-off than liquored up. I wasn't going to give Harvey another cent and apparently they weren't going to leave without either booze money or roughing me up a bit. If this was going to be my Waterloo, then better on my property so I could file charges later.

Where is a cop when you need one, I thought as one of Harvey's stooges threw a punch in my direction. It missed, but a shot from the second man glanced off my chin and staggered me back a step. The three of them reminded me of the crazed, living dead, out for blood and brains.

Just when I was prepared to retaliate and go down swinging, a gray blur dropped from the sky and attacked Harvey. A claw dug into one of his cheeks and blood sprayed from a torn flap of skin. I and the other two men watched in amazement as the bird fluttered and pecked on ole Harv's forehead.

"Christ " Harvey yelled and swatted the bird away, but the bird flapped in the air and swooped again, continuing his attack. This time, a chunk of hair and skin was dispatched from Harvey's scalp.

The fight amongst men had been forgotten, at least temporarily. When Harvey's goons hollered and swung at the gray crusader, he dive-bombed the three of them while crapping on one's shirt. The man waved his fist threateningly in the air. "Holy shit," he said.

He may be right, I mused.

The language directed at my bird was colorful to say the least. Every time Harvey tried to turn his attention back on me, he'd have to duck away from another low pass as blood dripped down his face and hung on to dead blades of grass.

"What's with that friggin' bird?" one of the men asked.

"Don't know," I replied. "Probably doesn't care for drunks."

"We'll settle this later," Harvey whined, his blood flowing without me landing a single blow, his eyes cautiously darting toward the sky.

All the neighbors within earshot were now standing at their front doors, silently witnessing the spectacle.

"You come back and I'll have the law on your ass for trespassing and assault." I didn't know if I could do that, but it sounded good.

As the terrorized threesome shuffled back to their beat-to-shit pickup, not only did my dirty bird flutter above their heads just enough to keep a stream of swear words floating through the air, but he had also managed to pile a load of his trademark green and black crapola on both side-mirrors.

***

The saying is: "All's well that ends well." I saw no more of Harvey and friends and you'll be happy to know I came up with a solution to my dirty bird dilemma.

Although the reasons or purpose for the events involving my feathered visitor were beyond my grasp, it was time to make peace. I confiscated two huge wooden freight boxes and screwed two shiny chrome side-mirrors into the wood. I moved the setup to the side of my house near the garage mostly out of sight from the street. I re-hung my bird feeder on a nearby tree limb and returned Mrs. Wallace's trap.

What could I do but accommodate my new protector who had saved me from a likely ass-whuppin'? I still haven't opened the windows to my house, however. I'm not willing to concede completely.

I've noticed also that I very rarely have salesmen or solicitors come to my door. Who needs a big dog or a "Don't Bother Me" sign when you have a small, gray, prolific pooping piranha watching your back?

Not me.

This contemporary story leads a gossip hound into more than he bargained for. It's a variation on a tried and true theme, but I believe the genre has room for one more interpretation especially within the gritty, pulsating backdrop that is New York.

Where The Gods Feast

John Jamison disliked being called J. J. and discouraged its use by the few people he considered friends. Like most New Yorkers, he had any number of grievances concerning the way life was as opposed to the way it should be, but on this day he ignored some of those irritants as he hurried along Fifth Avenue skirting the barricades protecting pedestrians from the white-hot sparks of a welder's torch near Forty-ninth. The pounding rhythm of a jackhammer assaulted one sense while the smell of giant roasting pretzels whetted another. *The grit of New York*, he mused. *Nothing like it anywhere else.*

Although his mood was upbeat as the result of a curious case just completed, the results of which he held inside a manila envelope, there was no intrinsic love affair between him and the city. If anything, a feeling of alienation had taken root. It was a sentiment similar to what he felt after he had been shacked up with some self-serving woman for too long, or the pang of culpability from some dirty job he had taken on. In fact, he was beginning to abhor doing what he was paid good money for: To dig up dirt on people who would prefer to keep their secrets buried.

Blackmail, plain and simple. By any other name, it would smell just as foul, but that part of the game was not his call. He left it to his clients to extract a payoff for reburying surreptitious activities. Once, all it took was a photo of a well-known personality smooching someone other than his wife on the Central Park carousel to land a substantial paycheck.

He saw little of the big loot, being no more than the middleman or go-between, the two-bit shamus that stuck the shovel beneath the surface persona, turned up the worms, and then passed them on to third parties to deposit in the right places. But, to balance his misgivings, Jamison had a weakness. He loved his electronic toys and expensive nights on the town enough to chase away whatever scruples he might have about his role in the universe. His greasy skullduggery for wealthy clients paid for extravagances his cruddy, everyday PI capers could never procure.

Jamison had brushed against numerous perversions and addictions in his occupation, but this case had a new wrinkle. This time around, his assignment had been some rich-bitch wife from uptown whom Jamison had candidly captured on film. She liked to show up at galas, premiers, charity functions—that sort of thing—but she also took pleasure in picking up bums off the street and rewarding them with a glance into a world that they had never imagined, experiencing brief but intense intimations of grandeur. That was her real charity work.

No hunky health club employee or cute waiter was enough to satisfy this affluent damsel. She preferred her pleasure down and dirty—some booze or drug infested low-life who most people would cross the street to avoid.

As Jamison strolled up Fifth, he observed the buildings across the avenue. His glance rose above street level, above the drugstores and T-shirt shops, to the corniced stone and filigree where

Old New York still survived. The shops at street level reminded him of his work, quick service and turnaround for the quick buck, of little value, nothing that would prove lasting or meaningful.

"What the fuck," he mumbled as he entered a revolving door just off Fifth that led to the man wanting proof of his wife's dalliances, a wealthy stock commodities husband, Bernard Dalworth II.

As he studied the light sensitive photos Jamison had taken of his wife dragging some rummy into a fancy midtown hotel in the middle of the night, Dalworth's nostrils flared, as if the smell from Vivian's companion emanated from the 8 x 10 glossies. "My wife, a woman of supposed class and breeding, seeking men off the street … the indignity of what might be taking place …"

Jamison stood quietly, noticing Dalworth's expensive designer suit with the pant cuffs breaking over just as expensive wingtips, while he allowed the big shot to contemplate he and his wife's future.

"I want something else from you, Jamison," Dalworth said with a sneer directed at the pictures, or Jamison, or both. "These photos beg for further investigation. I want you to playact. Make yourself known to her and see if she'll pick you up. I want to know exactly how far she goes with these skuzzballs."

"I don't think it takes much imagination to figure out what goes on behind closed doors," Jamison replied, wanting nothing more than the money he had been promised. "She's not running a mission."

"I've got to know to what level of degradation she has sunk."

Jamison didn't like the sound of it, but when Dalworth primed the pump by pulling a fistful of hundreds from a drawer and fanning them on the desktop before him, he reckoned he could stretch his talents to that of a street thespian.

"Double your fee for the pictures. Half now and half when you get inside with her and report back."

Half and half. That's the deal a customer that has watched too many private dick movies usually wants to cut, and Jamison was more than willing to take half the loot before providing the goods. "Sure Mr. Dalworth, half now and half later, if she'll pick me up, that is."

"I know you have the talent to imitate one the these cretins she's ... taking up with."

"I'll do my best."

***

Jamison quit shaving three days prior to Vivian Dalworth's next opportunity to prowl. A few rumpled clothes and he looked as down and out as any bum on skid row.

Like clockwork, Mrs. D. hailed a taxi around 10 PM. Jamison hailed another. The Indian cab driver made him flash some green before speeding off in pursuit of the first taxi. The cab followed her to an upscale restaurant/bar where Jamison paid the cabbie and waited outside in the shadows for an hour and a half.

Finally, Vivian emerged alone, a little unsteady but still looking like at least half a million bucks. Her body had a way of sending off a signal, and part of Jamison's body got the message posthaste. She hailed another taxi and he prepared to do the same, but the lady's cab simply pulled down a half block and idled.

Jamison watched the cab through a parade of passing vehicles and the plume of blue exhaust from the taxi's tailpipe. Vivian was watching the foot traffic apparently waiting to find someone to her liking, auditioning passersby.

Making his move, Jamison dodged traffic, crossed the street and sauntered up to the taxi's street-side passenger window. When he tapped on the glass, Vivian's head swiveled toward him just as the cabbie growled, "Get away, ya bum."

Vivian cracked her window an inch.

"I wouldn't do that, lady," the cabbie admonished.

"What is it?" she said to Jamison.

"Wondered if a swell lady such as yourself could spare a couple of bucks. I'm a little down on my luck at present."

She opened her dainty clutch bag and withdrew a five-dollar bill. "Will this help?"

"You're very generous." Jamison smiled. "Maybe someday I can do something for you?"

She shoved the bill through the narrow opening that connected her to the outside world where Jamison's fingers awaited. "I doubt that," she said abruptly and rolled up the window.

Jamison silently cursed himself for missing the opportunity. Perhaps he didn't appear down and out or filthy enough to satisfy this haughty woman's craving. The capricious nature of his chosen profession and, in the end, the meaninglessness of his actions pummeled him again. There was nothing to do but walk away.

"Mister?" Mrs. D. called.

Jamison turned.

Vivian had rolled her window down all the way this time and motioned him back.

"What now, bitch? A refund?" he muttered soundlessly.

"That was awfully rude of me. Let me give you a lift."

Jamison's attitude changed as quickly as a glitzy marquee flashed from one color of light bulbs to another. He danced on the inside but didn't want to appear too enthusiastic. He slowly walked around the rear of the cab, cracked open the door then hesitated.

"Don't you have somewhere you need to go?" Mrs. D.'s voice had taken on an edge of laughter.

"Sure I do ... usually ... just not tonight."

"Get in. I won't bite. I know a place you can stay and obtain some good stuff to drink, unless you would rather blow your five bucks on rot gut?"

Funny, Jamison thought, that she would assume his proclivity was most likely alcohol. He guessed she had found booze to be the drug of choice among the street lice. Like Vivian's husband, he was becoming increasingly curious about how her walks on the wild side played out.

Mindful of traffic, Jamison opened the door and climbed in.

Mrs. D. gave the driver an address. He stared through the rearview at the odd couple, but apparently had been driving long enough to witness about everything the backseat of a cab in New York could offer. His interest soon abated.

"My name is Juliana," she said.

So the cat and mouse starts with aliases, Jamison pondered. *Smart of her.* She didn't ask for his name but Jamison said, "Mine's Pete."

"Well, Pete, this could be your lucky night." She turned toward him, lowered her chin and produced a teasing little smile. "Ever spent the night in a penthouse?"

Jamison looked into her gray eyes and fought the urge to say, "Yeah, a time or two with babes just as hot as you," but instead said, "I don't mean to be disrespectful, but this is only a temporary situation with me. You don't have to do me any favors, really."

"I see. A noble man, temporarily on the skids." Her tone wasn't so much condescending as it was unconvinced. "I think you'll do just fine. I need a little help myself tonight. Perhaps we can assist each other."

She turned her head away and appeared interested only in the streets ahead. For several blocks, the city's flashing lights, its noisy lullaby and the hum of the taxi's wheels kept them company. Jamison studied the woman's profile as it turned light then dark then light again as storefront lights swiftly crawled inside the cab and disappeared just as quickly. He wondered how far he wanted to play along with this nympho, or whatever she turned out to be. It could be fun, lots of fun, but the money was more important than this skirt. Plus, he was supposed to report her predilections to the husband. Taking a proactive part in this discovery might be frowned upon as well as costly.

The taxi pulled in front of a hotel where Jamison had seen Vivian take men before. She paid the cab driver.

"Come along," she told Jamison and he obediently followed her past the doorman, whose palm she greased with a twenty.

She said no more until an elevator had whisked them to the top floor and she had waved him through the room's double doors. "I promised a penthouse," she said following him in.

"You certainly did, Juliana." He walked through the well-appointed space to the picture windows that extended the length of the room. The view revealed the Empire State and the Chrysler Buildings along with other Manhattan landmarks in all their multicolored glory, topped off by a crescent moon that floated between skyscrapers.

Suddenly Vivian was at Jamison's side to admire the city as well. "The place where the gods feast," she said as solemnly as if they had entered a church.

Below lay the circadian rhythm of glittering sprawl and moving headlights, a miniature etching in motion—bright, seductive, full of both promise and sorrow.

"The devils feast here also," he added, transfixed by the superficial beauty mixed with the ugly underbelly he knew to exist within the colossus. Still looking at the panorama of light, he asked, "So what am I doing here?"

"I think you know."

"But an uptown girl like yourself? Why pick up a guy off the street like me?"

"Let's just say I like the earthy type. Let's say the earthier the better."

She stood close to him. He thought they were about to kiss but instead, she put her face near his chin and smelled him. "You haven't been on the street long. Maybe you *were* telling the truth about not being a chronic loser."

He turned quickly and grabbed her shoulders. "Do you get

your kicks from playing this little game of 'rich broad shows charity to some low-life bum?' I'll probably be happy to play along if you'll tell me what the game involves?"

"That's fair ... Pete ... is it?"

"Yeah, it's Pete." He released her and stepped back, realizing this had become more than a job. Although truly enthralled, almost desperate to discover what made this particular variety of female tick, he was not about to lose sight of the payoff. The money was far too good and Dalworth was far too important to let his sudden lust for this *femme fatale* take him anywhere but out the door and as soon as possible.

"Go to the bar and make us a drink, whatever you prefer. Let me step into the powder room and freshen up, then I'll show you what I like to do and how I like to do it."

"You want me to clean up a little?"

"You stay just like you are, but don't forget the drinks."

He had broken one of his own rules by not carrying the piece he normally strapped to his right mid-calf. The challenge of this caper seemed little more than whether or not he would be keeping his clothes on. Staying dressed would make it easier. *Nothing too bizarre*. She'll want to be whipped, spanked or have degrading sewer language spewed at her, or some other variation on a theme. Or maybe she wants to get off by licking the street off of him? He would let it go far enough to uncover an adequate amount of stink before he made his apology, hit the road and eventually reported to Bernard Dalworth II as to what variety of thirsty kink his lush wifey likes to imbibe.

He carried the drinks to a coffee table and sprawled on one of the penthouse's sofas. He looked for the moon which had disappeared behind the top of a building with only its opposing tips visible on either side of the spire, like two sharp teeth and waited with anticipation for the Queen Bee to reveal her true identity as Batgirl.

"Where the gods feast, my ass," he said softly, a slight grin curving his lips. He reached for the solace of his scotch and took a long sip, enjoying the smooth burn in his throat and the spreading warmth alcohol provided.

Finally, the bathroom door creaked open. Vivian stood within. The trained lighting on the expensive foil wallpaper bathed her with a soft golden backlight. Jamison could see only that she stood naked, a silhouette of near perfection. She stepped over the threshold and came to him. The reflected light from the skyscrapers painted her faultless torso in pinks, whites and blues.

Vivian picked up her drink and swallowed most of it. She towered over Jamison, the intensity of her desire palpable. "Mmmm, a scotch man," she breathed.

Jamison sat his tumbler down. His gaze was riveted on the smooth lines of the body that encompassed a close-cropped triangle of dark velvety hair that rested tantalizingly at eye level. *A body to die for*, he thought. "What now?" he asked.

"Not much, just a kiss on the neck." She sat on his lap and nibbled around the scruffy three-day-old stubble.

When she moaned, his hand couldn't help but seek one of her hard, tactile nipples. There had to be more to this than a slow burn leading to straight sex. If he had to feel her up for a while … well … it was part of the mission after all, the path to unresolved questions.

She shifted, placing her knees on either side of his hips, straddling him, her generous lips returning to his earlobe, neck and shoulder. The position gave both of his hands the opportunity to explore her. He took to the task with enthusiasm, but maintained his resolve to make this short and sweet. "All right, sugar. I'm a little old for a hickey. What would you have me do?"

Without a reply, Jamison decided to get up from under her and force the action. But then, he saw something that momentarily constricted his movement, freezing him in place. Something startling and unexpected. He closed his eyes tightly and opened them quickly to make sure he was not hallucinating.

Another silhouette stood between Jamison and the bathroom's glow. It glided toward them. Jamison pushed against the woman draped over him, but she was like three hundred pounds of lead, an immovable object, attached to his neck like a gigantic leach.

Dalworth II himself, adorned only in a pair of boxer shorts, now stared at the odd couple in a tug-of-war of sorts on the sofa. A warped, sneering smile not unlike his wife's, cracked his otherwise austere, businesslike countenance.

"Look who's here," he announced by way of greeting. "You see, Jamison, when you're married to a she-devil like Vivian, you have to make certain concessions."

Jamison again pushed against the taut, naked body facing him, but he might as well have been pinned to the mat by Hulk Hogan. How she managed such strength was merely one of many fractured half-formed questions floating beneath his skullcap. He looked at Dalworth, then back at Vivian who had, at least temporarily, come up for air. In spite of her copy-written sardonic smile, she looked different. A white flame danced in her eyes, while her expression slowly changed into something rather unpleasant.

"What's the deal here, Dalworth?" Jamison shouted not giving up on his attempt to crawl from beneath the woman with superhuman strength. "Does she do things to men while you watch?"

"That's one way to put it, old chum. You have little choice but to go along with rather crude methods of entertainment when you live with a beautiful, insatiable blood-sucker."

Jamison looked at Vivian again. He could clearly see the elongated teeth beneath the wicked smile. Fear gripped him the way smog grips a city.

"I'm not so perverted, am I?" Vivian said with a pernicious

pout, almost a purr. "I'm not going to have sex with you or abuse you in any way. I'm only going to suck a reasonable amount of blood out of you. Not enough to kill you, just enough to give you the gift."

Jamison tried to strike out with his fists but Vivian was too quick, a skilled defender, warding off the blow rendering it harmless. Freeing himself from Vivian's death grip became an exercise in futility. He instinctively reached for the leg weapon he had never needed until now, yet knowing it was not there. A prayer sprang from the mind of the suddenly repentant man, a prayer that all of this was just a horrible dream or the result of a cannoli gone bad, but he retained the clarity to know what was happening was as real as his file on his present client's wife, to be disposed of sooner than expected. The luminescent crescent on the canvas of night was now impaled by the skyscraper spire, captured by an uncaring, unforgiving city, as was he.

There was nothing left to do but scream. One long burst followed by a short one that came out as a pitiful cry.

"No use." Dalworth smiled snidely. "Not up here in the penthouse, above the city, above everyone and everything but us. Up here where the gods feast."

So terror waited at the top of the metropolis for the chosen ones as well as it did on the skin of its teaming streets. "Why me?" Jamison wailed.

"Simple," Dalworth continued. "She finds men that no one takes notice of. In your case, we needed someone who performs your kind of unscrupulous dirty work in the event anyone becomes suspicious about our nocturnal escapades."

Jamison stared at Dalworth.

"Oh, don't be so thick. That intuition or sixth sense some investigators posses I didn't sense in you, and I was obviously correct. You didn't seem careful enough, a little sloppy; maybe you don't care for your work anymore. Whatever the case, we are your salvation. You'll be one of us now and you'll do anything to protect what we have, what we crave, including taking care of snoops if necessary. The thirst is all that will matter and, of course, the desire to please. You have no one that's close. You won't miss the old way and no one will miss you."

"I lied. I do bite," Vivian told the helpless man pinned beneath her as she attached her face to his neck once again, this time in search of a large vein.

Jamison flinched at the sharp sting of Vivian's penetrating fangs. He heard the gurgle of his blood entering her mouth and the half crunching, half smacking noise that rose above her joyful, thankful moans.

"Just squeeze her breasts until she's finished," Dalworth advised. "It will help give you a sense of familiarity and calm. Like mother's milk for the both of you."

Jamison's strength and will to resist evaporated. He did what he was told as he gradually slid downward into whatever realm of existence these two beings might bring forth. Before his vision faded, the final scene transmitted to his brain was that of the huge fangs sprouting from Dalworth's gums.

"Not too much now, dear," Dalworth II said to Mrs. Bernard Dalworth II with the pure glee of anticipation. "Save some for me, before he slips into the arms of Morpheus."

***

John Jamison doesn't go out much anymore except on those special occasions when his new job requirements make it necessary. He now has meaning in his existence and a desperate goal. His PI business, money and his old pursuits for pleasure have become irrelevant as others now pay his room and board. He waits only for the tap at his door that tells him one of Vivian's street people or one of Bernard's hookers has brought along a friend ... someone to suck on, and it is his turn to feast as do the gods that own him. He is slave to these moments that satisfy a hunger more addictive than street drugs. The Dalworths had cured Jamison's self-pity by making him one of them. And now he was infected by the cure.

And there are those rare occasions when the creature at the door is none other than Vivian. He does not mind that she has taken to calling him J.J. or the dangerous new assignments he is sent on for she is the one who made him what he is, the one whose breasts he delights in kneading while she takes more of his blood, the one who trapped him into becoming a part of her guilty pleasures, the one he exists to please.

This dark tale is about a young woman caught between the surreal worlds of dreams and nightmares. She revels in her newly-found good fortune while a specter lurks, waiting for the unexpected moment to strike. Laura's voyage pays homage to old movies, exotic places, and romance ... before it all goes wrong, that is.

Laura's Dream

A chamber in Laura's heart holds something frightening and hungry, a huddled image in a corner of her existence, a dark side. Clearly etched, it hovers on the fringes of her thoughts, a gloomy premonition Laura can't escape—a macabre movie scene from Hitchcock.

The image is simple enough, a scene in black and gray, right off the movie screen into her world.

A distinguished man holds a woman in his embrace.

"Time's up," he whispers to the woman. "And sweet dreams."

The man looks over the woman's shoulder at Laura, who becomes the object of his attention. He gives her a curious, yet cunning smile. Something cruel and feral lurks within that smile, something that smacks of death and destruction. Something in the man's expression tells Laura her wonderful existence is at an end.

Her longing for a movie career keeps the specter at bay, stopping it from intruding on hard work and good times. And yet, it never leaves her. Not completely. It lurks in the subconscious.

But as the train whisks her from Nice to Lyon, Laura's life is good and optimism fills her dreams. She has met a man who has swept her off her feet, a man whose experience and persona might be powerful enough to exorcise that pesky premonition.

Outside her compartment, the French landscape flies past blurring shades of green and gold. As the sun nears the horizon, she focuses on Paul and their *rendezvous accompli:* a weekend of unbridled, unparalleled passion.

Woven into the fabric of her dream stands the image of Paul at the train station moments before, bundled up against the late afternoon chill, waving to her. Her desire and caring have grown with each encounter. She holds tightly to those feelings as she stares out her window. The sun drops ever so quickly behind the crop fields and orchards, taking the fall colors with it, creating an unhurried fade to black.

Laura wills her unpleasant black-and-white, movie-like vision to stay on holiday. She'd much rather think of walking through a French village, hand-in-hand with Paul, in a world where colors change hue.

She recalls their trip to the *Costa Brava* and her first weekend with Paul. Running along a warm, deserted beach, they'd thrown themselves on the white sand, stripped off their wet bathing suits and made mad, passionate, refreshing love.

"I never dreamed it could be like this," Laura had told Paul, as they lay naked and wet, without shame. "We're like Burt Lancaster and Deborah Kerr in *From Here To Eternity*."

"With the raw verve and zeal you possess, my sweet, I'd have to say our lovemaking scene is more suited to an *Emmanuel* film."

The next day, they had made love near a jagged cliff where there were rocks and currents. The waves mimicked the ebb and flow of their passion—a splendid spot to release sublime emotions strong enough to test the world's synchronicity. In this harbor—the safe shore of Paul's arms—the tentacles of some unknown terror would not be able to reach her she felt certain. These moments with this savior, the movie star and the man, were fulfilling her untamed dreams and keeping her specter far, far away.

Laura has been held by the Silver Screen images for as long as she can remember. She related to Scarlet O'Hara's independence and later, in college, to Katherine Hepburn's hard-nosed "professional woman" roles. Movies convinced Laura she was destined for something beyond the limits of her small, dull hometown.

As a teenager, she had allowed the high school sweetheart to grope her at the picture show while she dreamed of being on film with the matinee idol. But she remained steadfastly free of promises and silly commitments. She wasn't about to be trapped by a homegrown, clumsy kid and the little ones that would follow, not with the world as her stage.

Laura watched her movies and hungered for her opportunity, the exciting life she had so often seen on-screen, a life filled with adventure and romance.

Her chance had come with a fellowship to study acting in France. In the time it took to rehearse a scene, she had packed her dreams along with her wardrobe and was on her way.

Now she lives with all the *joie de vivre* a twenty-two year old, vivacious budding actress can muster. "And, I have Paul," she murmurs with a flicker of anticipation for the thrill of their next rendezvous.

They had met at an outdoor café complete with pigeons. Laura had sat alone in a plaza in Lyon near an ice cream stand, studying and daydreaming as accordion music floated tenderly on an afternoon breeze. Paul had been sitting two tables away reading *Paris Match*. Her ice cream dripping onto her textbook had brought him to her rescue.

Paul was astonishingly handsome, graying at the temples and looking enough like Louis Jourdan to make her stare unabashedly. He was a man with a mysterious job for some Parisian firm.

In spite of her incurable romanticism, Laura knows their relationship is only a brief whisper in time and space. But it will be a moment she can always cherish when it finally ends, when new roles will send her in new directions.

Paul was an open, warm man toward whom women gravitated. And it was France, after all, and she has become a liberated woman, thanks to him.

"When we are together, we make love first," Paul seductively said after their first holiday. Reckless abandon intertwined with waves of passion carried her away to another place, a Technicolor world with Dolby sound. Paul has created a hunger inside her, a hunger and thirst that can never again be quenched by hometown traditions and taboos.

"You are the most exquisite of jewels, *mon cherie*," he said after they made love as she had never known love before. They had laughed with delight as their liaisons often culminated in screaming orgasms she had only imagined in her dreams.

The fact that Paul sometimes became remote after his warm, final tremor of release only added to the thrill, making the moment more like a script written for a Calvin Klein *Obsession* commercial than one from her beloved forties flicks.

In Paul's arms, she had truly evolved into a woman of the world, no longer an ingénue. *I have a full-blown romance with a debonair European who coaxes from me the most beautiful music with sensitivity and magnetism,* Laura daydreams.

Laura has waited her entire existence for this role and she loves playing the part.

***

As the train clickity-clacks through the French countryside, Laura watches farmhouses rush by, silhouetted by the sinking fireball behind them. Her eyes focus on her reflection in the window glass. She has gotten prettier during the past few weeks since the make-up people have worked on her, especially during her scenes with Paul. She has almost become her character. It is her love interest that has transformed her and she wishes the shooting would never end.

Snuggling against the side panel of her seat, she dreams about her next encounter with Paul, the man she feels can chase away her frightening vision forever.

At the next stop, she hears footsteps in the passageway and hopes desperately to keep the compartment to herself.

Finally, the train lurches away from the station. Her door clicks open. She keeps her eyes closed and lets her consciousness drift, determined not to let the intruder distract her from thoughts of being cradled in Paul's arms like a romantic scene in the classic movies she loves.

As the train enters a tunnel, something causes Laura to stir. She opens an eye slightly to see who her fellow passenger might be. In the dim light, she sees the shape of a person seated across the cabin.

Something strange yet familiar about him. She opens both eyes. Backlight captures his form as well as that of another, a second shape superimposed over his. The two people are in an embrace. The temperature in the cabin drops drastically. Something is amiss. She senses ... What? Dread? Danger?

Her train car clears the tunnel. The remaining glow from the west provides little light, but enough to see who sits across from her: A man. His eyes riveted on her.

With the woman still in his embrace, the compartment's overhead lighting spotlights his face. A face Laura knows as well as Paul's. A face from the place of dreams and nightmares ... an apparition she had hoped would never again darken her path.

The grinning man.

The woman's back is to Laura. The two figures are drawn so closely together she cannot distinguish between the two. She is dressed in Laura's clothes.

LAURA'S DREAM

"This can't be," Laura breathes, sitting upright, fully awake. "It's all wrong."

Laura and the man stare at each other. The wry grin creeps across his face, turning into a leer, hungry for her. He lacks color. Rather, he is tinted silver-gray, just like her dream scene, just like an old movie. She watches, mesmerized, as he removes something from his overcoat.

Scissors.

Laura's hand flies to her mouth, too stunned to move or speak. *Is he going to kill the woman with those scissors? Is that what's going on?* She is terrified. Her nightmare has never gone this far. If only Paul was here to save her. She surrenders to the fear and tries to rise but an unseen force pins her to her seat, her body unable to obey her command.

Laura recoils against the seat cushions, hoping somehow to escape through the paneled walls of the cubicle. The scissors flash in the dim light, the steel blades reflecting off her corneas now bulging from their sockets. She is horrified, yet transfixed.

No. He's not stabbing the woman. He's cutting something ... pieces of film falling to the floor.

Up and down the scissors fly. Snip, snip.

But why? Why is this woman in my clothes? There's nothing like this in the script. Why?

Snip, snip. Celluloid floats down like feathers.

"No ... It can't be me. Don't take my dreams. I want to be with Paul. Please, not now ... Not after coming so far "

* * *

"You sure that's necessary, Al? Cutting her like that? It'll change the whole sub-plot."

"The girl's got to go. The storyline can survive without this chick screwing Paul, although she's a real piece of work," Al says, grinning.

"You're the editor," Max replies, disappointed but resigned. "I feel for the writer though, trashing his girl-becomes-a-woman bit."

"That's showbiz, Max. He'll never admit it, but he's better at writing his *film noir* stuff than sex and romance." Al snips the last piece of celluloid. "Goodbye, Laura and sweet dreams."

A few years ago, my son asked for my help with a school assignment. Always eager for the opportunity to do something different, I offered him a brief, thrown-together screenplay of the scenario below. He and his acting/film crew received an "A" and I quite liked the resulting two-minute movie.

Shadow Boy

Shadow Boy rolls his bicycle tire between two iron poles in front of his middle school. He does this with relish knowing the day has arrived when accounts will be settled. His shadow has told him, "After today, no one will pick on you or call you names ever again."

He marches into the school, passing other students scurrying to their first classroom. A few of them take long enough to say things like, "Hey four-eyes," or to bump him and say, "Watch where you going, loser."

The tardy bell rings and Shadow Boy plunks down into his seat just in time.

"Glad you could join us today, Billie," Mrs. Sullivan says.

Everyone else knows him as Billie Tunstill, but he knows his real name is Shadow Boy and today is the day his tormentors will not soon forget.

A piercing scream from the hallway interrupts Mrs. Sullivan's role call. "Stay in your seats," she orders her students while she peers into the hall. Ms. Gault is hovering over a girl. Mrs. Sullivan runs to see if she can be of assistance while Mr. Morgan comes out of his classroom and joins the small group surrounding Mary Lindsey.

Mary reclines against a hall locker clinching her side. There is blood on her hands.

"My God, what happened, Mary?" Ms. Gault asks.

"Something stuck in my side," she sobs.

All three teachers look and see a large, metal nail file protruding from Mary Lindsey below her ribcage.

"Call an ambulance," Mr. Morgan tells Mrs. Sullivan as he takes Mary in his arms and quickly trots toward the nurse's station.

"Billie Tunstill was here," Mary cries. "I didn't see him do it, but he was here."

Mrs. Sullivan returns to her classroom to put down a small rebellion. "Billie, step out in the hall for a moment," she says, keeping her voice steady, calm.

"If something's wrong, it's doughboy's fault," a student says from the back of the room. Mrs. Sullivan does not admonish the student. She has too much on her mind at the moment and Billie Tunstill does seem to be in trouble regularly.

In the empty corridor, Mrs. Anderson states, "Mary Lindsey was hurt down the hall a few moments ago, Billie. She says you were there. Did you see what happened?"

"I didn't see anything. I was hurrying to class."

"Did you stick her with something? It'll be easier if you tell me now."

"I said it wasn't me. I bet she's not hurt that bad anyway."

"How would you know?"

"Well, she's so perfect."

Mrs. Sullivan resists the urge to slap Billie. "All right. Someone else will probably want to speak with you about this."

Billie regards her with no change of expression.

Mrs. Anderson sighs and leads him back to class where paper airplanes and spit-wads are once again sailing through the air.

A stir of excitement pulsates through the students when the ambulance parks in front of the school and takes Mary Lindsey away for treatment and observation, but by the conclusion of lunchtime, the students and staff return to their customary routine.

The hallways are quiet again until Teddy Long, the ordained future terror of the high school gridiron, stumbles into the building from the playground.

"I ... need ... help ... *Somebody!*" he screams with a mixture of pain and anguish.

Once again, a teacher appears from his classroom and observes Teddy Long drunkenly staggering down the hallway, his hand over the right side of his face, blood oozing between his fingers. The teacher runs to his aid and forces Teddy to lie down on the scuffed, green linoleum.

Teddy is shrieking and crying at the same time. "My eye " he bellows. "Stuck in my eye."

The teacher becomes aware of a black and white BIC ballpoint pen between two of Teddy's bloody fingers. Other teachers and students steal out of their classes and approach the scene. Most turn away after a look at Mr. Touchdown's punctured eye socket filled with blood. Ms. Gault heads for the telephone this time.

"Stay calm, Ted," the teacher consoles.

"*My eye!*   " Teddy Long screams louder than before. "Billie Shithead. He saw who it was."

"Billie Tunstill? Did he do this?"

Teddy can hardly get words out between spasms of pain. "He was standing in front of me. Why didn't he do something?" Teddy wails.

Billie does not join the pandemonium now taking place in the hallway. Instead, Mr. Morgan takes him from his classroom and stealthily escorts him to Principle Phillips's office. While the commotion continues elsewhere, Shadow Boy waits patiently, grinning slightly.

Eventually Mrs. Somerville, the school district's psychologist, walks into the principal's office and closes the door. "Hello, Billie."

Shadow Boy does not answer.

"You've been in this office quite a bit during your two years here, haven't you, Billie?"

He still does not answer.

She pulls a chair in front of Billie and sits down. "You've been teased a lot haven't you? You feel like there's nobody to stand up for you? Isn't that it?"

He is quiet a moment longer then says, "I have someone to stand up for me." His eyes meet the psychologist's for the first time. "People won't hurt me anymore."

Mrs. Somerville raises her eyebrows. "Who might this person be?"

"Someone that knows how to get even."

"There's been quite a bit of excitement at school today and you know the reason, don't you, Billie? Both children say you didn't do this to them, but you were there and you can tell me who it was, who this protector is."

Shadow Boy grins conspiratorially, making her uncomfortable.

"You can't hurt who did it and if I tell you, you'll try to have me locked up or something."

"I'm not the one who decides what to do about your part in this, but as for who your friend is, try me. You might be surprised at the stories I've heard from students."

"It's my shadow that does it," Billie says abruptly. "He follows me and sometimes does what I think about."

Mrs. Somerville tries to control a smirk. "C'mon Billie, you can do better than that. I've talked to you before about fitting into the school and I know you aren't delusional. You just have an inferiority complex you'll soon grow out of. When you get to high school and find other kids with your interests ... well ... that's not what we have to discuss today. You have to tell me exactly what happened to Mary and Ted, for your own peace of mind."

"I already told you, it's my shadow."

"All right, Billie. I don't know whether you're searching for attention, or sympathy, or what, but I think a policeman wants to talk to you next. Are you sure you don't want to tell it to me first?"

"My shadow will look out for me."

Mrs. Somerville exhales heavily, places a notepad back into a folder and gets up to leave. She looks at Billie one last time as he sits placidly in a chair. As she turns to the door, she notices a shadow on the wall, a silhouette of Billie coming toward her. She turns again and sees Billie still in the chair. She looks back at the wall just in time to see the shadow holding a pair of scissors above its head and plunge them downward into her shadow. She screams too late.

"People just don't listen to me," Shadow Boy resignedly utters. "My mom and dad didn't listen either," he tells his shadow as he scrambles out the office's window while wondering how many more people will suffer its vengeance before someone catches them both.

It might not be a tale told on Brokeback Mountain, but once Jed and Sinclair both become aware of the strange cactus berries, their lives most certainly take an unusual twist.

A Tale For The Trail

"'May the demons of hell rise up and devour all of you,'" the woman screamed, her face plum destroyed by grief as she held what was left of her husband. There wasn't much. His thick old tongue hung out of his mouth. His eyes bulged out of his skull, darn near. His throat was almost cut through, the way I heard it. His head darn near came right off in her lap as she sat there rocking him back and forth, a half dozen Injun arrows sticking out of him ever which way."

Jeb took a sip from his tin coffee cup. "You tell a pretty good story, Sinclair. Tell it real fancy like you've had a heap of book learning."

Sinclair smiled. "Just because I punch cows or do a little stealin' doesn't mean I'm a half-wit, but it's not Injuns I'm scared of. There's not a man alive I'm afeared of. It's something else. Something that changes you. Something waiting to get inside."

"Like poison from a snake bite?"

"Naw, it's something you don't see until it's too late." Sinclair drew a long swallow from his own cup then flung the grounds beyond the campfire's glow into the dark.

Jeb studied Sinclair, his features dancing and changing shape from the firelight. He looked like a statue hunched over the campfire, like a wise man lost deep in thought and it irritated the hell out of Jeb. "You got something more to tell me or can I roll over and try to get some shuteye?"

Sinclair grinned slightly. "I got something to tell. Besides what else we got to do out here in the middle of nowhere but sleep or tell stories before pushing on to Armadillo?"

"Why do you always say Armadillo instead of Amarillo?"

"I like to play with words. Gives me something to think about between towns besides looking at stars and listening to the coyotes."

Jeb was tiring of Sinclair's meanderings and stretched out on his bedroll. As for himself, he did not think about much of anything between towns besides how long their poke would hold out before they had to pick up a job or rob somebody to pay for whiskey and whores. When he and Sinclair finally got sick of each other's company, they would ride their separate ways and hitch up with other drifters off a trail drive or off activities less honorable.

"You haven't been this way before, have you, Jeb?"

"Can't say as I have. Why?"

"Cause this story I'm about to tell happened right around these parts. It wasn't just something I heard neither. I saw it with my own eyes."

Jeb was not going to ask again. Sinclair could fuck himself if he was going to play riddles when they both could be sleeping. They had been in the saddle three days under a sun drenched sky and the more Jeb thought about it, the more he wanted to partner up with somebody a little less talkative than Sinclair.

"This used to be Injun country and anytime you're in Injun country, you hear stories about spirits and burial grounds and such."

Jeb had been on the trail long enough to hear his share of tall tales and hoped Sinclair would not rattle on much longer. "Just tell your stupid story, take a piss and bed down, will ya?"

"See if you think it's stupid after you hear it. About three years ago, me and two other ole boys rode this way after leaving a herd in El Paso. We were going to ride to Tulsa, but all of us never made it that far."

Sinclair stopped talking long enough to rearrange the red-hot embers that were once tree limbs. The reconfigured firelight cast dancing shadows on the nearby rock formations and sagebrush. Sinclair almost looked like some old craggy-faced, Indian medicine man leaning over a fire, trying to make contact with the spirits of his ancestors.

"This something I was telling you about. The thing I said could put fear in a man? It was on this kind of land that I first saw it."

"Sinclair," Jeb said, his voice sounding tired and less tolerant, "If you don't tell me what the fuck you're talking about right now, I'm going to carry my bedroll somewhere else where I don't have to listen to your yammering."

"That would be a bad idea, son. I'm sort of sneaking up on this story because it's a lot for a man to take in. The only reason I'm telling a pup like you is because you're a lot like one of those boys that rode with me that other time."

"Whaddayamean, like me?"

"Oh, he was young, kind of cocky, didn't have much patience with things, but he was the first to notice the Injun beads."

"Beads?"

"They aren't really beads. They're berries. I heard tell the Injuns in these parts plucked them off cactus and strung them on horsehair. Made necklaces out of 'em."

"I ain't never seen berries on a cactus. They's blossoms."

"That's what made these different."

"What's that got to do with something inside you?"

"See, that's what I mean, Jeb. You have no patience with nothin'. I'll tell you what happened, but you have to let me tell it in my own sweet time, 'cause it'll take time for you to understand."

Jeb placed his hat over his eyes to cut out the fire's red-orange glow. Maybe he could doze off while Sinclair ran off at the mouth with this fool story.

"So me and these two cowpokes come through this area and one of 'em ... his name was Billy ... he sees these berries growing off a cactus plant. That crazy kid would eat anything including trail plop if he was hungry enough. Anyway, he starts eating these berries and the other guy tells him they might be poison. Crazy Billy don't give a shit 'cause he's hungry."

Jeb peeked out from under his hat to see why Sinclair had stopped talking. He had stood up and was looking out across the dark horizon like he was seeing it for the first time.

"Go on, dad-burn-it."

Sinclair sighed. "That evening we camped out, sort of like you and me are doing now, and ole Billy starts to complain about feeling funny. Like he's seeing things and all. They call it hallucifyin', or something like that. All of a sudden, he hops up off his gear and starts attacking Len and me ... the other guy. We try to get him down but he was crazier than a shithouse rat. He was foaming at the mouth and trying to bite us and I swear his teeth had grown real long and sharp like a wolf or bear or something. He just wouldn't stop and he bit Len a good one. He had a hole clean through his arm." Sinclair went silent again.

Jeb rose up on his elbow. "Damn it, Sinclair, what did you do?"

"We had to shoot the son-of-a-bitch. All we *could* do."

"I don't get it. What did him going crazy have to do—"

"What it had to do with them berries, my friend, is they's

what done it. I found out later that the Injuns used to eat them before a battle. Made them fight like devils and gave them a craving for human flesh."

Jeb stared at Sinclair, seriously at first then a smile carved its way along his lips. "You must think I'm the dumbest pecker-head ever put down. I ain't never heard *that* story."

"That's because, as far as I know, we were the only white men to ever try them berries and I had a chance to see if it's true."

"So you got more of them?"

"Yep. Picked some off a cactus yesterday while you was relievin' yourself or playin' with yourself or whatever you do on them walks. When I cooked up the stew tonight I made two batches, cut up the berries and threw them into one batch. How you feeling anyway?"

"What?" Jeb sat up. "I don't believe one damned word, you crazy, good-for-nothing drifter. Why would you want to make me like that?"

"You been getting on my nerves lately, Jeb. If them berries work, I'll have to shoot you, take your goods and tell the sheriff that you went crazy after eating yourself a handful."

"I feel just fine. You're the one you need to be worrying over, thinking I'd fall for something this crazy so I'm going to laugh—ha, ha—and now I'm getting some sleep." Jeb lay down and placed his hat back over his eyes. "Eat berries and grow teeth," he muttered. "Crazy dookie-tasting varment."

Sinclair walked over to Jeb, picked up his rifle and pushed Jeb's hat back with the toe of his boot.

"What the …?"

Sinclair stood over Jeb with a strange crooked grin. "I'm not through telling you my story. I come back through here last year just before we met up. I found out it was true what I heard about them berries."

"You let somebody else eat them and took their grubstake?

That's mighty low if you did that." Jeb rose up again a little afraid of Sinclair now and wondered if his partner had gone loco. "Why would you go and tell me if you were gonna' bushwhack me? You wouldn't need to feed me no berries and I'm not letting you pull a fast one on me."

"You don't understand, Jeb. I didn't feed you any Injun berries. I ate 'em myself. Now do you get it?"

"Stop this crazy talk." Jeb looked at his rifle.

Sinclair tossed it beyond reach. "I told you all this because it takes some time to work. I have to feel it coming on and it's so much more gratifyin' when you smell the fear in a man." His voice had grown rough and slurred. It throbbed in Jeb's ears like the beat of an Indian drum. Jeb wanted him to stop saying these things. He wanted him to stop talking altogether.

Before Jeb could get to his feet, Sinclair shoved him to the ground with the sole of his boot. A wider grin covered Sinclair's face and it looked to Jeb like his teeth had grown and sharpened. His gaping grin was now a slobbering leer.

"Human meat tastes better than anything you can imagine, Jeb." Sinclair spewed saliva while his long tongue darted from one side of his canine features to the other. He pounced on Jeb, tearing into the jugular with his snout of serrated teeth.

Across the still prairie, with only a few hills and ravines to break the whine of the wind, another howl accompanied those of the lonely coyotes.

I would like to think this tale is in the tradition of the old Alfred Hitchcock Presents series. It's a tale of strange bedfellows; one above ground, one beneath it, and when a third party enters? Well ... three's a crowd.

Houseguest

He listened to Emily's footsteps move purposefully across the kitchen floor above him. In twenty minutes, her automatic garage door would grind open and her car engine kick in. Then the house would be his again for nine to eleven hours depending on how late she worked. He waited another five minutes to make sure she did not forget anything, but she never did. Emily was a creature of habit, the most organized person he had ever happened across. He supposed that was what came from living without people or pets.

He had never seen Emily, but figured she was one of two women in a photo that stood on her dresser. There were no pictures of men or children, so he further assumed she had never been married. Her wardrobe belonged to a woman no younger than forty, someone who worked in an office and did not go out much.

The few times he had heard Emily talk on the phone, he could not make out the conversations, but they were usually brief. The most telling characteristic about her was that she never had company, not in the two months he had lived in the crawlspace beneath her tidy ranch-style house. The doorbell sometimes rang, but the people on the other side of her threshold must have been salespeople, the pizza man, or beggars like himself. A pizza delivery was a special treat because Emily invariably left a piece or two inside its box in the garbage.

His new life had begun in November. Cold and hungry, Emily Preston's back door lock had been easily disengaged. He had not known Emily's name then. That came later when he saw her junk mail and bills on the kitchen counter. There had not been much worth taking inside her tidy house, but in a storage space off of her bedroom, he had found entry to a twenty by twenty crawlspace. He shone his penlight into its corners and found the space dry and free of pests, as tight as a concrete bunker ... or a tomb. He would risk spending the night.

The following day, after Emily left for work, he climbed out and raided the refrigerator. Emily's house was small but cozy. He had owned a home once, before his life fell into a downward spiral, before jail time. He made the decision to stay another night, so he put back the food exactly as he had found it—shy a few slices of bread and lunchmeat. The crawlspace beat standing at an interstate off-ramp with a cardboard sign, and it sure beat the hell out of fighting for a bed at the shelter.

Two nights became three, then six, then two weeks. After a month, he lost his fear of discovery. Emily left every weekday at the same time and never returned home till six or later. He developed his own routine. He bathed and shaved every few days, washed his few clothes, took just enough food from the pantry and fridge not to be noticed, and lounged around the house watching TV or reading. Emily subscribed to enough news magazines to stave off boredom. Creating a comfortable place to sleep had been easy—stolen lawn cushions and old blankets from Emily's highest storage shelf, his extra layers of clothes, and his winter coat provided reasonable accommodation.

His primary daily duty was to be certain the house appeared to be just as Emily had left it. That included washing dishes or silverware he used, replacing ice cubes, wiping down every place he used water, and smoothing out the sofa cushions and her bedspread, where he sometimes reclined and thought about his life.

Just before six, he watched the driveway until her car pulled in and then he quietly descended into the crawlspace and closed the trapdoor behind him. The house to which he had grown accustomed remained Emily's domain at night.

He had found a spare key and made a duplicate, but the only time he felt the need to leave was Thursdays. That is when he disposed of his accumulated trash and hit the interstate to collect money for extra treats—a fast-food burrito, candy, a beer now and then—food to get through the weekends when Emily stuck close to home. On Thursday nights, Emily went out for some kind of meeting so he could return after dark and crawl inside his makeshift bed before she came home.

Night after night, he lay in his crypt-like space listening to Emily's soft footsteps paddle from the kitchen to the living room to the bathroom and waited to hear the water from the toilet or sink or tub run through the pipes and wonder what she would do if she knew he listened below. There was something comforting about her movements and the sounds, even that of the furnace cutting on and off, providing heat for the woman only a few feet above him. They were sounds of a normal life.

Then, on a Saturday morning, the trapdoor flew open and Emily quickly descended the four steps. He tried to retreat into the concrete wall, tried to make himself invisible, but Emily did not glance in his direction. She sat a canister in the middle of the room, pressed a button, then departed, closing the door behind her. The canister fizzed, releasing an unpleasant chemical cloud that soon assaulted his eyes, ears, and throat.

"Bug Bomb," he whispered.

He had to stop the spreading gas or get out. He crawled to the canister and threw his heavy coat over it, then bolted for the way out to take his chances on discovery. His hands pushed against the plywood trapdoor, flipping it open. He climbed the steps and tentatively looked into the bedroom and adjoining bath. Emily was nowhere in sight. He had not heard the garage door or her car, but in the confusion, he may have missed the familiar sounds. He stealthily slipped from room to room. When he was certain she was gone, he recovered the canister and tossed it in the back yard where it could fizzle and die.

When his eyes quit burning, he looked at Emily's kitchen calendar. A neat line was drawn through five days. Above the line, she had written, "Sister." He grinned at the thought of having the place to himself for five days. He would panhandle until he had enough to get some extra food and maybe he would sleep in her bed. There would be plenty of time to be topside as long as he kept the lights low and cleaned up carefully prior to her return.

After three days, he knew it would be hard to go back into the crawlspace but, at the same time, he had grown accustomed to Emily's habits. She never talked to herself, but occasionally hummed along with the music she played. He missed the sounds and he missed her. He had only seen her that one time, in silhouette, when she released the bug bomb, but she looked determined—a no-nonsense person who took care of business. If he slipped up while she was gone, she would notice and surely call the cops. They would find him and drag him away.

Through the edge of the curtains, he watched a neighbor pick up Emily's paper each morning. The time had come to move along, but he could not bring himself to do it. The holidays were near and Emily would play Christmas music and there might be treats she would bake for her office or bring home. He wished he could see her face and wondered which of the women in the picture was she and which was "sister."

He came uncomfortably close to getting his wish upon Emily's return. The garage door clattered open while he dosed in front of the TV. When he realized what was happening, he clicked the TV off and flew over the couch making a beeline to the safety of the trapdoor. He stumbled, almost knocking a lamp off its stand, steadying it as the garage door closed and the kitchen door opened. He scrambled to his feet and reached his hiding place in time, praying she did not notice the *wumph* of the plywood door as it dropped snugly into place.

He backed into his secret corner and listened. He heard a man's voice. Emily and the stranger were laughing. Someone has come home with her. That might be a blessing. It will keep her from looking around too closely ... but ... what if he stays? *Not Emily. She's not the type to bring someone home.*

The man's voice grew louder as he tried desperately to hear their words.

"I'll set these in the closet for now," the stranger said.

He heard a bump on top of the trapdoor.

Luggage. The man had placed luggage on top of his escape route and left the room. There was nothing to do but wait. He hoped the stranger would soon leave and Emily would go to bed and everything would be as it had been, as it should be. He wrapped himself in a blanket and waited for what seemed hours with only the sound of distant mumbling to keep him company. Then he heard another sound. Emily was sobbing. He had never known her to cry. *Who was this person in the house with her? What right ... ?*

A shuffle of footsteps came into the bedroom. He could make out the stranger's words once more.

"It'll be okay, Emily. Just lie down and relax."

For the first time, he could hear Emily's words clearly. "This isn't right. It's been years. I need time."

"This is the time," the stranger told her. "What difference does it make how long it's been? Just take it easy."

He listened carefully, hanging on every sound above. The words had stopped. He imagined what was taking place and felt like crying himself.

"No!" Emily screamed.

He heard what sounded like a slap followed my Emily's wails. She was being attacked. He could not squat down there and just listen. He had to do something. He crawled to the trapdoor and gave it a push. It did not budge.

The goddamned luggage.

Emily screamed again. This time it sounded like one last wailing plea.

"Oh, shut up," the man told her. "You've been without it too long."

On the steps now, he put his shoulder to the door and pushed for all he was worth. He heard the suitcases slide. Another shove and the door opened. He scrambled up the steps, out of the storage space behind Emily's closet and into her bedroom.

In the dim light, he saw the stranger tearing at Emily's slacks and underwear. She was pinned by his forearm as her arms flailed at him.

He ran to the bed, hooked his arm around the stranger's neck and pulled back. "Stop it," he screamed as he saw Emily's face for the first time. It was streaked with tears and one side was reddening from the slap. He pulled the man off of the bed and pushed him away.

"Who the hell are you?" the stranger gasped, holding his tortured neck.

"You better get out of here."

"I'm an old friend," the stranger said. "We were just playing around ... "

"Please leave," Emily pleaded.

The stranger looked at him. "I've got more right to be here than you. Where the hell ... ? You were hiding in the house. Do you even know this person, Emily?"

"Please go, both of you!" Emily said, pulling her torn blouse over her chest.

When he turned his attention to Emily wanting to explain, the stranger threw a sucker punch, sending him sprawling on the floor. Emily screamed as the stranger placed both hands around his neck and squeezed. "You're an intruder. You're the one that doesn't belong, you asshole."

He was close to losing consciousness from the pressure of the man's thumbs when he saw Emily looming over them. She held a large object and crashed it against the stranger's skull. The man slumped and fell to one side.

"Thank you," he croaked, his vocal chords straining to make sounds.

"He was trying to kill you," Emily cried. "I had to do something."

"Of course you did."

Her ripped blouse hung loosely from her shoulders but she did not care about that any longer. She looked very fragile as she sat on the edge of her bed and dropped the marble bust of Beethoven that had torn open the stranger's skin and cracked his skull. "You're the man from the crawlspace," she said matter-of-factly.

"Yes," he said, "but how … ?"

"I've always known you were there. I'm a bookkeeper. I count things. I'm very efficient that way … and the little hairs around the edge of the sink. I knew you weren't here to harm me and now, thank God … "

"But the bug spray?"

"I didn't want you thinking I was suspicious and leave. I knew you'd get out of there once I was gone."

They both looked at the man who lay face down in a spreading pool of blood.

"He's not … No, he can't be," Emily said, fresh tears welling in her eyes.

He had seen death before and this stranger, this man who had conned Emily in some way, had come to cause harm, to take advantage, was most certainly dead. He looked at Emily and nodded.

"Oh my God," she said. "I didn't mean to ... I had to stop him."

"You did the right thing."

"He lives near my sister. We went out years ago. Said he wanted to look for a job here. I gave him a ride." She covered her face with her hands and sobbed.

He stood next to her and placed his hand on her shoulder. "I know what to do. It'll be all right. I can take care of this. You aren't to blame. Will you trust me?"

Emily looked up at him. "I trusted you to stay in my house," she said softly, wiping her tears.

"Why? If you knew, why—"

"Because I was lonely. As silly as it sounds, I took comfort in you being down there. I was about to be brave and acknowledge you when I had to visit my sick sister. I decided to wait till I got back and if you were still here ... " She took his hand. "Now it seems there was a reason for your being here. What's you're name?"

"What was that guy's name?"

"Bill Jacobsen."

"Then call me Bill."

***

"It looks like him. This is his spot and them's his clothes."

"You have any idea who would want to do something like this?" the detective asked the transient.

"Hell, who knows? I never even knew the guy's name. He hadn't been around so much lately."

The detective sighed, put his notebook in the breast pocket of his jacket. He knew the investigation would come up empty and that this John Doe might never have a name.

***

Bill and Emily spent their nights together listening to music or watching TV. She cooked for him and he kept house. He intended to look for work as soon as the holidays were over. They knew they would always have each other, their secrets safe in each other's arms.

Emily called her sister to tell her how much Bill had changed and how well things were working out. "I'll come visit after the holidays," Emily told her. "Now that I have Bill to take care of things, I can get away more often."

Written mostly for laughs, this tale shows that terror may take root in the most unexpected places and at the most inopportune times.

The Man On The Bathroom Floor

In this age of Jesus sightings in a potato chip or the Virgin Mary on a piece of French toast, Alice supposed she should not have been shocked to spot a man's face in a linoleum tile square residing between her feet in front of the toilet bowl. "What the shit?" she exclaimed, literally the appropriate remark.

Alice is not senile. She is a twenty-five year old female with a pixie face, a good body and most of all, perfect vision. She has often been told by members of both sexes that she is "hot" for whatever that is worth.

Young or old, eyes dilate while engaged in stationary activity such as taking a crap. They lose focus and spot all sorts of images on textured walls and in complicated patterns, especially while engaged on the throne when the mind seeks far away places as the body completes its digestive process.

This time was different for Alice, however. She focused on an image of this man, amazed she had never noticed him before. Her interest increased as details emerged. Although her bathroom tile pattern monotonously repeats every second tile, this particular square varied slightly from all the others in the most enticing of ways.

The image was most unsettling. The man's pallor was pale and unearthly—that of a starved miscreant. His eyes were deeply set. One openly glared while the other was shut, but that one black, empty, glaring eye ... God help her ... was an abhorrent, unnerving sight, a window through which Alice saw no compassion or remorse. The mouth snarled, revealing jagged teeth, poised to take a fleshy bite from her bare ankle.

This demon on the floor looked more sinister than your run-of-the-mill monster, more heinous than what you might see on the cover of a horror comic book.

An alarming twitch took root in Alice's toes, ran up her legs to her groin. She instinctively spread her feet farther apart, away from this figure that might possess an ability to leap from the confines of a trivial piece of assembly line plastic and rubber, and take her from the rational world where she was presently occupied with the one activity—a healthy dump—in which people know exactly what is required. A fear heretofore unknown swallowed her as if the creature on the floor might engulf her while she sat, putting the finishing touches on the job she had come to do. She willed her eyes away from the laminated tile square, flushed the toilet and hastily left.

Although Alice did not consider herself a person to sail away on flights of fancy, the next few times that duty called, she took along reading material. It did not help much for she knew the man on the bathroom floor was between her feet, looking up even if she did not see him, perhaps studying her painted toenails or lusting after the parts of her that were beyond his view, winking with that second closed eye.

She did not mention this phenomenon to anyone. If she were to comment on what she thought she had seen, there would be no end to the raised eyebrows and catty smirks. "A frustrated, fertile mind hungry for an adventure," her girlfriends would say.

In the ensuing days, Alice forced her mind to be less imaginative. Her significant other had been to business meetings all over the country for two weeks, so she focused on his return. The evening he arrived on Alice's doorstep, they briefly hugged and kissed before he made a beeline to the little room that held the scary man on the floor.

If she were to make a serious comment on what she saw, John would tease her unmercifully. Maybe even laugh at her. Instead, Alice teasingly called out from the living room, "See anything interesting between your legs?" She smiled to herself and added, "On the floor, I mean."

He did not respond. Then she heard a whooshing sound of air rather than water and a loud thump. That was all.

"Are you all right?" she called, making her way to the bathroom door.

No response.

Alice shoved the door open and found the room empty. A pounding migraine immediately tortured her brain and the room felt as if all the oxygen had been sucked from it along with whatever living, breathing organism had been foolish enough to enter.

There was but one piece of evidence that John had ever come home and disappeared into the privy. One tiny drop of blood ... one tiny drop, lying on the tile at the base to the toilet bowl. And the drop had fallen in the face of the man on the floor. And the face seemed to grin a little. And just maybe there was something else; something in the tile canvas that could have been a second face below the first, its mouth possessing the shriek of terror and eyes bulging in unrelenting torment.

**

Why the monster in the bathroom took John, Alice may never know. "Maybe if she had not called attention to the man on the floor ... hadn't acknowledged him?" But what good did it do to speculate on a world beyond our understanding.

When John's friends and family call, Alice tells them he never came home. What else can she say?

"Should I move away or stay?" Alice often asks herself. "What if the usurper on the floor can somehow restore John to me?" These are thoughts she ponders as she uses the bathroom now, never looking at the tile floor but not covering it with a throw rug either, for that might block the portal for John's return ... or possibly her future entry.

This tale tells of a young girl caught between the worlds of brutal reality and her whimsical fantasies, a victim to powers beyond her control that lead to an inevitable destiny. The surreal adventure pays homage to something that seems out-of-date in our modern world, yet still holds magic and charm for some.

My Pretty Painted Pony

In twenty years, the Right Reverend Smiley Gunderson had found many an unexpected item residing on the top step of his small church, but nothing to rival the squirming infant in a bassinet. A note was pinned to the baby's pinafore. It read: *This is Becky. Please find her a home.* Short and sweet.

Smiley Gunderson was not inclined to take in an additional mouth to feed, but he did not believe it was Christian to turn an unwanted child over to strangers. He dutifully took little Becky home to the angst of his overworked wife with her passel of screaming brats—two boys and two girls, to be exact—and promptly turned the duty of raising "God's gift" over to his dutiful wife.

Becky spent the next six years being, at best, tolerated. The Gundersons fed and clothed her, but the milk of human kindness was woefully shallow. 'Out of sight, out of mind' was the policy toward her.

Just after Becky's seventh birthday, Mrs. Gunderson died suddenly. The gossip in town favored the opinion that her four monsters and her husband, who had perfected the art of dodging chores by disappearing on church business, drove her to an early grave.

The four Gunderson children were shuttled off daily to a church school, and Becky began her unhappy association with other children in the first grade. Children can be cruel and poor Becky paid the price, being outfitted with third generation clothes and questionable credentials. But, she soon found an escape.

For years, the town fathers had threatened to tear down the deteriorating old carousel that resided in the far corner of a triangle of hard-packed clay and sparse Bermuda grass commonly known as City Park. But, like most committees, they never seemed to come to a decision about much of anything. It was at this ancient carousel that Becky took refuge.

Reverend Gunderson had never cared much about Becky's whereabouts and when his wife passed on, he cared even less. Consequently, Becky found herself in front of the old merry-go-round once or twice a week at first. Soon, she was there daily. As the afternoons grew shorter with the coming of winter, she would stand and watch the horses and wooden seats made into swans spin slowly, hypnotically.

She had no money to ride, but she knew which horse was her favorite. It was a gray appaloosa with a spotted rear end. She wished she could mount him and ride until the image of the school, the house she lived in, and the questions about her origins were swept away with the swish of her pretty painted pony's black-hair tail.

One day, George Sinton, the old man who ran the carousel, took pity and invited Becky to ride for free. There weren't many kids around anyway since the town counsel had allowed the carousel to fall into disrepair, channeling funds instead toward a shed of cheap construction for the town's maintenance vehicle.

"Come on over, young lady, and take it for a spin," he said to Becky.

Even though the carousel was as shabby as Mr. Sinton, Becky

did not notice. She ran excitedly to the carousel entrance, quickly hopped upon the wooden platform and made her way to her pretty, spotted, painted pony. She hugged his neck. "Oh, I'm so happy to meet you," she said into the chipped black enamel eyes.

"Get on and hold tight, girl," Mr. Sinton commanded.

It was a tough job for a little girl no bigger than Becky, but she managed to scramble into her painted pony's saddle as the old man pushed his button and pulled the lever. The merry-go-round started to move. As it picked up speed, Becky was transformed into a world of peace and beauty. The painted scenes on the music pavilion merged into a trip through a green meadow next to a lazy, blue river, all the while astride her gallant, dappled steed. Glass mirrors above the scene reflected a wonderland of sparkling light through convex prisms.

Becky squealed with delight as she rode around and around, carried through a utopia of freedom and tranquility. She reached forward and petted her pretty painted pony's scraggly black mane. She had never felt so happy or so close to anything. Becky and her pony rose and fell as she held tightly to the brass pole. Up, down, then up again.

"I could ride you forever," she told the piece of wood, scarred by decades of children and teenagers climbing up and down. The paint on his prancing left leg was completely worn off from shoes perched on top of it, but Becky did not care about his imperfections. He was beautiful and the only horse she ever cared to ride.

Her pony's up and down motion suddenly slowed. The ride was coming to an end much too soon. Becky wondered if she stayed put and did not move, maybe Mr. Sinton would forget to tell her to get off. She held tightly to the brass pole.

"You have to get down now, young lady. We've got other riders," Mr. Sinton called out.

She climbed from her mount. "I'll be back, pretty pony. I'll get some money so I can ride you again ... some way."

Becky's eyes shyly met the old man's. "Thank you for letting me ride." A craggy smile cracked his weathered face.

The calliope music of the carousel haunted Becky as she walked away. She could not bear to look back, afraid one of the riders would be seated on *her* pretty painted pony. Other horses on the merry-go-round were white. Some were jet black, many with bejeweled collars. Maybe *they* would appeal to the other kids that came to ride. She and her pretty pony with the spots on his behind belonged to each other.

That night, Becky dreamed of riding her pony through the meadow along the babbling brook toward an inviting farmhouse with smoke billowing from its chimney.

The next day, although hesitant to approach Reverend Gunderson about anything, she asked if she could perform some special chore to earn a little change. There was something about the way he had begun to look at her lately that made her uneasy, but she was desperate for money, and she had learned from life's hard knocks the talent of deception. She could mask her fears and insecurities at school or at home when she had to. This time it did no good, however, as Mr. Gunderson grunted something unintelligible and waved her away.

Becky supposed it was no wonder the only father figure she had ever known was grumpy. She had overheard a neighbor lady discussing his habit of frequently sampling the communion wine while his own children ran wild. Perhaps that is why he had some bad habits.

At school, she talked a classmate out of a quarter. Maybe that would be enough to get another ride. She could only hope Mr. Sinton would accept a single coin. He seemed kind enough.

When the school bell rang, Becky ran the three blocks to the city park, to the little triangle of land tucked in the corner of the park where she knew her pretty painted pony would be waiting for her.

But something was different today. Mr. Sinton was dragging a sawhorse in front the carousel entrance creating a barrier. Becky approached him warily. "Excuse me, Mr. Sinton," she said anxiously. "I have a quarter." She held it up so he could see. "Could I please have a ride?"

"Sorry, little lady, but the town's shutin' us down. They say we're relics."

"But ... "

"Yeah, tearing 'er down," he went on. "Progress they call it. They say kids don't care for things such as this any longer, and even if they did, town ain't spending the money to fix 'er up. Probably put up some plastic piece of junk. Don't know what I'll do. Will be pickin' up trash around it, I suspect."

Becky could not grasp all of what Mr. Sinton was telling her. All she knew was she had a shiny coin and her pony waited patiently. Wasn't he going to let her ride after all? Her lower lip quivered and her tear ducts were on the verge of opening.

Mr. Sinton looked at the child for a moment. "What's your name, young 'un?"

"Becky. Becky Gunderson."

"The preacher's kid? I heard about you." He studied her for a moment. "Tell you what, Becky. They may be shutin' us down, but were not plowed over yet. What would you say to a ride ... a long ride ... a ride like no other kid has ever had?"

Becky looked at the old man and wondered if he was teasing her since he "knew who she was" and all. She again held out her coin.

"You keep your money, child," Sinton said with kindly eyes. "Go pick out the horse you want and we'll have us a time."

Becky could not believe what she was hearing. She smiled broadly at Mr. Sinton, shoved the coin in her pocket vowing to give it back to her schoolmate, and ran to her pretty painted pony. She could swear it smiled just a little as she approached.

"Hello, my pretty pony." She put her tiny cheek against her

pony's black nose then quickly placed her worn-out tennis shoe on the dirty brass foothold protruding from her horse's tummy. It took all her strength to pull herself up into the saddle, but she eventually straddled her mount and waited. For a moment, she was frightened Mr. Sinton had changed his mind, but the merry-go-round finally started to move.

"You ready to ride, Becky?" Mr. Sinton called while piddling with the controls. "You ready to ride non-stop till they come and make us stop?"

Becky squirmed with excitement and squealed. The old man took that as a "yes" and cranked up the gears.

She felt her pony rise and pick up speed. She had no problem returning to her fantasy world where her pretty painted pony was alive and carrying her across the meadow toward the faraway mountains. Around and around they flew … where they would stop, nobody knew.

Becky thrilled to every revolution, but knew the time with her painted pony would soon be over. Still they had gone around many more times than the usual ride. Maybe Mr. Sinton meant it. Maybe she could ride until someone made him stop. "Oh, if we could only go on forever, my pretty boy," she gleefully shouted.

Around and around, up and down. Becky caught sight of Mr. Sinton. He was having a good chuckle as if he were enjoying Becky's ride as much as she.

Then something happened. There was a flash of light and a pop above the carousel near the enclosure where Mr. Sinton sat at his control. He looked to see what had occurred. At the same time, the carousel began to accelerate. Faster and faster Becky, her pony, and the other horses raced.

Mr. Sinton was yelling something at her. She did not understand what it was, could not know that her uninterrupted ride had caused old wires to overheat, creating a short.

Faster and faster they flew like a spinning hovercraft about to lift from its mooring and rise into space. Mr. Sinton was in quite a state. He was waving his hands wildly at Becky with each spin of the carousel. She heard him this time.

"Get off, girl " he screamed. "Jump ... now "

But Becky held on to her pretty painted pony's brass pole as they sped faster and faster. She was not afraid. She was safe on the back of her pony because she knew he loved her as much as she loved him. They were going so fast now it seemed they would soon tear free of the pole that was bolted at top and bottom. They would fly above the clouds that were already forming around them. The mirrored glass on the music pavilion now looked like glittering stars as they merged into a solid stream of reflective sunbursts.

Becky couldn't hear Mr. Sinton any longer. All she knew was that her painted pony's mane had grown long and luxurious. His dull gray paint was now muscled flesh and supple hair. His saddle was of the softest leather she could have imagined. "Oh, you're real " she exclaimed. "My real pony." The brass pole was gone now and she held onto her pony's velvet reins as he whinnied and galloped at a smooth gate so that Becky's ride would be cushioned and perfect.

They were headed into the sun as Becky's eyes watered in the bright light. But that was all right. She knew her pony would take them to the meadow with the river and the mountains beyond. She knew she would never see Mr. Gunderson, his bratty kids, or the schoolhouse again. She and her pretty painted pony, no longer paint and wood, but flesh and bone like her, were all that mattered. And that was enough.

✳✳✳

George Sinton told his sad tale to the investigators. "I tried to get the child ... Becky ... to jump off the thing, but she paid me no mind," he lamented. "It happened as quick as a wink. The short in the wires caused the undercarriage to overheat and the whole shebang was in smoke and blazes in no time." He lowered his head. "That poor little girl. She just wouldn't get off that horse."

"We've gone through the ashes, Mr. Sinton, and there's no human remains that we can find. Are you sure someone was riding? Maybe she got off and ran away and you didn't see?"

The two men in suits looked at each other slyly. Mr. Sinton knew what they were thinking: Here's an absent-minded, stained skivvies, drool case that gets mixed up easily and wouldn't remember one child or one ride from the next. "She was on the carousel, I tell ya," he said flatly.

"Okay," one of them said, smiling. "We have no more questions for now. We know this is a sad day for you, sir. If there's anything we can do?"

How about giving me back my livelihood and giving that little girl her life back, he thought but did not say.

"Take care then."

The two men walked away. There was no one now. The firemen followed by the gawking locals had all left. Mr. Sinton was finally alone with his thoughts. "Damndest thing," he muttered, looking at the carnage that remained. "Make the counsel happy. Be easier to bulldoze now that … "

The next word caught in his throat. He walked closer to what was left of the carousel, which wasn't much except for a painted panel of the music shell. On the scene's peaceful landscape, the fire had left its blackened mark. The mural was unharmed except for a single flaw. But it was not a flaw at all. It was a perfect silhouette of a happy little girl riding her horse across the meadow toward the welcoming farmhouse.

Mr. Sinton's face cracked into a grin and tears weld in his tired eyes. "No wonder they found nothing in the ashes," he said to the surrounding trees and the squirrels inhabiting them. The old man who thought he had seen it all removed his sweat-stained baseball cap. He wiped his brow and his lower eyelids. "Nothin' to find. Little gal's in a better place than this. That's for sure."

This fantasy/Sci-Fi piece came to me during a time when I needed eye surgery. With a twinge of wonder, it tackles the issue of what might become of us if our world suddenly went dark.

Dancing With A Blind Girl

Bodies whirled and twisted on the dance floor to the booming beat of *Play That Funky Music, White Boy.* The blind girl sat at a table with a girlfriend and her seeing-eye dog, tapping her foot to the rhythm.

"Would you like to dance?" I asked.

She looked in the direction of my voice. A smile crept across her face, an honest good-natured smile that more than offset her unfocused gaze.

She didn't know whether I was short, fat or ugly. All she knew was someone had asked her to dance.

"Go ahead. I'll watch Bandit," her friend told her.

Some inflection in her friend's voice must have told the girl I was presentable, but I don't think it mattered. Her Golden Retriever lay patiently under her table, out of the way. His soulful brown eyes looked unsurely at the stranger who'd asked to borrow his mistress. The blind girl patted the dog's head and I led her toward the small square of hardwood on the lounge's dance floor.

"I'm not very good," she said.

"Neither am I. What's your name?"

"Beth. What's yours?"

"Spence."

The pounding beat ricocheted off the walls. Most everyone in the lounge was up, their feet gyrating in personal, frenzied interpretations of a fertility dance.

"I think we have a little room to maneuver here," I shouted.

She smiled trustingly and began her own variation of booty shaking. With her arms raised above her head, she resembled a Spanish *Contessa* clicking castanets, enjoying the freedom of her own space.

"You move beautifully," I told her.

She didn't answer. She was caught up in the rhythm of the song, appearing "normal." Her enthusiasm was contagious. I moved as sexily as I knew how, forgetting my efforts were lost on my partner.

Finally, the white boy was no longer playing the funky music.

"Thank you, Spence." She reached out and touched my arm to show her appreciation and to give me the opportunity to lead her back to Bandit.

A slow song wafted from the speakers—*Unforgettable*.

"Are you all right with one more?" I asked.

"A tummy tickler? Sure I am."

She melted against me the way every man hungers for, clinging like a vine long familiar with the stone it intertwines. Her head against my shoulder, she hummed along with the music.

Other couples swayed languidly. In that moment of closeness, I considered how attuned her remaining senses must be without sight. When the song ended, I guided her back to her brown-eyed boy who waited expectantly, his muzzle resting on his paws.

"Thanks again," Beth said.

Her friend gave me a curt smile as I ambled back to a corner of the bar feeling I'd done my good deed for the evening.

Beth and her girlfriend finished their drinks and left. I would never see her again but I often thought of how adept she'd been at making the most of her situation, how her blindness didn't interfere with many of life's pleasures. It was an important and ironic lesson because within a few days, I would be as blind as she.

*＊＊

It started for all of us on August 3, 2008. My alarm sounded at 6:45. I slapped it off and kept my eyes tightly shut, seeking a few more precious moments of quiet, holding a job I'd grown tired of at bay.

But the world wouldn't wait forever. I rolled over expecting to witness the sunlight streaming through my bedroom window.

Nothing but darkness, not even a shadow, as if our sun had abandoned the galaxy, the thick blackness of the darkest night imaginable. I closed my eyes tightly and then rubbed them with the heels of my hands.

I opened them again. No reassuring golden glow, only the gloomy nothingness of a coalmine deep in the bowels of the earth. My hands reached out with fingers curled into claws, as if I could pull away a black shroud of extreme night and reveal the familiar world of light and images. I grasped only air.

Then I panicked. My hands waved wildly, knocking a picture of Mary Ann from my nightstand. I heard the glass crack as it hit the floor.

I flailed in the emptiness, not knowing what to do next. Then I fumbled for the telephone next to where Mary Ann's picture had been. I felt for the numbers and dialed 911.

Busy signal.

I tried Mary Ann's number. Only her recording answered.

My emotions warped beyond panic to a deeper plane of terror. *Am I in some kind of limbo, perhaps dead, where darkness was a perpetual companion?* "It must be a nightmare, has to be," I said, willing my words to be true.

I would have screamed if someone on the street hadn't beaten me to it. The piercing squeal came from somewhere beyond my realm of imploding anxiety.

Banging my shin on a piece of furniture, I felt my way from bedroom to hallway, my arms extended like Frankenstein's monster. I realized I was crying. *What kind of cruel joke is Mother Nature playing?*

I thought of the blind girl I'd danced with ... Beth. I pictured her poise and grace. For her, just another day was beginning. For me, my life could be altered forever. Today could be the precursor to the end of the world.

My blind journey continued as I stumbled through a house no longer familiar toward my front door. I negotiated the passageway with a spastic dance step of my own, trying to think positive. *Maybe this is just some freak, temporary thing?*

Then I heard another scream. "I'm blind. Oh God, someone help me," a woman cried from somewhere.

Had a mad scientist gone Stephen King's "super flu" one better? Had some third-world demigod released a poison agent that first stole your sight and then took your life? Blindness might just be the start. My thoughts were racing helter-skelter, out of control. Something had gone hideously wrong and thrown my world into the blackness of sight and mind.

I felt for the bolt on my front door and forced it open. The earth had turned toward the morning sun after all. Although I couldn't see, its resplendent rays warmed my face and the deep blackness lightened a shade to dark gray. "Thank God for the sun." I began to have hope, thinking this condition might be improving.

The woman's voice again, screaming. It sounded like she had stopped in my front yard. *It could be my neighbor, Emily, the one who likes to play the Blues on hot summer nights.*

"Who's there?" I called out.

"Spence? I'm blind."

The most ludicrous thing I could've said would be, "so am I." It was too insane, too impossible. "Talk to me," I said. "Let me come to the sound of your voice."

This horrendous phenomena wasn't mine alone to bear and I took a measure of comfort in that. I wasn't isolated. Feeling for the woman, my arms moved to the right and left as I slowly approached. I ran into something and almost stumbled. It was the woman, kneeling in my driveway.

I dropped to a knee and put my arm around her. "It's all right," I said ludicrously. "I have you."

"I can't see " she wailed.

Her warm tears fell on my knee. I was as naked as a frequent dream. I'd have a jolly time explaining this to the cops if they showed up. But my thoughts were still in terms of a normal world.

"Is it you, Emily?"

"Yes," she said. "Can't you see me?"

"No, I'm afraid I can't."

"What's happening? Is everyone in this town blind?" she screamed.

"Let's go inside. I'm squatting here in my birthday suit. I'll try to call someone."

She reached out and touched my bare chest to confirm my statement. We stood and I found my way back to my front door with Emily in tow.

Another person yelled from down the street. At first I thought he'd seen me in the buff and threatening to call the police. Then, I realized his wails entreated anyone to call the police, as his eyesight had abandoned him.

I ignored his shouts and led Emily to my sofa. Feeling around and finding the telephone I knew to be in the kitchen, I tried 911 again.

I'm sorry. We are unable to connect your call at this time. Please try again.

Trying to put the phone in the pocket of my nonexistent robe, it only slid against my tingling thigh.

"What has happened?" Emily asked for the second time between gasps for air.

"I don't have a clue." I dialed Mary Ann's number once more and this time she picked up. "Mary Ann. Are you all right?"

"You mean, can I see?" She hesitated then added, "Have you turned on a TV or radio?" Her voice was strangely calm, frighteningly so. "It's worldwide. The whole world has gone blind, Spencer. The entire world."

I do not know how long I sat on my sofa after placing the phone on its cradle, or how long I listened to Emily sobbing before she wandered out of my house to return home, I presume, to contact her own friends or family. I know it was long enough to listen to CNN trying to make something rational out of the irrational. I listened and listened. Finally, I felt my way to the refrigerator and wondered how long my food supply would last.

***

Then the madness began—the madness of a world thrown into darkness. Life as I knew it had ended in the blink of an eye, so to speak. Fashion, sport, traditional warfare and commerce ... all vanished in an instant. The scientists squabbled and tried to find the mysterious genetic code that had swept across the face of the earth, but to no avail. The teaming masses, now in a world where prestige, power and appearance no longer mattered, prayed for salvation. Those who were blind before the apocalypse became the gurus of the future. And life went on.

***

It took a while, a great while, but eventually seeds were harvested and distributed to all who could find their way to the distribution centers—all those who had weathered the necessary adjustments and had chosen to keep living.

Existence had become basic and unfettered. My former manicured yard became home to a patch of earth that contained carrots, potatoes, tomatoes, and onions just for fun. Things I could feel. Things for Beth and me survive on.

As I said, I never *saw* Beth again but I did find her. She had been helping out at one of the indoctrination centers. Believe it or not, she recognized my voice. By some twisted quirk of marvelous fate I'll always be thankful for, we became a couple.

All of us still had music stations and talk radio, but I didn't listen much, except when someone came on to tell us how to do something, the blind way, to make life a little easier. But I had what I needed ... all there was *to* have.

***

Beth put a Blues ballad on the music machine and returned to the porch next to Bandit and me. I'd become fascinated by the heartfelt lyrics and liquid rhythms of the songs. I have poor Emily to thank for my learning the meanings behind the music. She'd just disappeared one day like so many others had. Lost, dead, or just moved on, who's to say?

My relationship with Mary Ann had shattered as thoroughly as her picture on my nightstand. Much about her had been based on appearances. I hoped she could find a way to live with the new reality of "being."

"Have you heard what they're saying about the latest vaccine?" Beth asked me. "Early tests have shown slight movement can be seen for up to twenty minutes with each dose."

"Where have I heard that before? Stay tuned," I replied as I found her hand and brought it to my lips, kissing it tenderly. "Did I ever tell you about the time I danced with a blind girl, before all of this? She was happier than me when I could see. Now I understand what blindness strips your life down to: the awe and wonder of someone's kind word or touch, without barriers. I guess the word is dignity. That's what she had—personal dignity."

I could sense Beth blushing as she nestled into the space between my arm and chest. "When I first lost my sight, I cursed when I dropped something," she said. "Then I learned to rejoice when I accomplished some little task." She turned her head and kissed my neck. "It doesn't really matter whether you see again does it? Not really?"

"We always want what we can't obtain. That's civilization's way. If suddenly there's a serum, I'll be the first to get in line. But I can tell you that for the first time in my life I'm content with who I am and what I have."

"Me too," Beth replied as unseen twinkling stars gathered overhead, their pinpoints of light beaming from suns burned out millions of years before.

I looked into the heavens. Even though I couldn't see the stars, I knew they were there. I still felt their magic and wonder even though I could only imagine them. I thought about my fellow humans feeling their way along, looking for meaning in their forever altered lives. "Here we are on this blue bauble in a sea of night," I said to Beth. "It still turns as it always has and the universe doesn't care if its creatures have eyes or wings or dreams. Everything just is."

The heartlessness of the human condition is exposed in this dark corner of civilization when a husband and wife are reunited. A dusty, desert town suggests caution to those that travel alone.

Detained

The street looked like a movie set. Tumbleweeds had found homes in front of a gas station, the Sheriff's Office and two other buildings that stood on opposite sides of the wind-swept two-lane blacktop. The town could have been deserted for all the life Sam could see, which was no life at all.

"The only way in hell Sara would stop here is if she was running on fumes or had to pee, or both," Sam muttered, stepping out of his car. He wondered if the wind always blew like this. The decaying automobiles and a few scattered trailer houses strewn across the landscape were the only windbreaks in this sad and lonely place … and these four pitiful brick buildings on either side of the highway.

Sam shielded his face from the swirling sand and debris and walked into the Sheriff's Office. An officer with a crew cut and a thick neck looked up at him from behind a desk.

"I'm looking for Sheriff Layton," Sam declared.

The officer twisted his neck a half-turn. "Sheriff" he shouted out the side of his mouth. His head swiveled back and trained on

Sam who tried to act nonchalant in the dismal two-desk office.

A tall, well-built man entered from a rear door. "What's the problem?" he asked. His gunmetal gray eyes seemed to burn a hole through Sam.

Sam fished a typed letter from his pocket as the man approached. He handed it to the sheriff who studied the note and nodded sagely.

"Well?" Sam said.

"Well what?"

"You sent this letter about my wife."

"Guess I did."

Sam's mouth formed a begrudging, crooked smile. *He's going to play games with me, drain it for all it's worth. Play me like a bass on the business end of a slippery hook.* "Look, Sheriff, let's work this out so Sara and I can be on our way. If I could see her, I'd appreciate it."

Layton smiled. "Okay, Sam Bingham from Scottsdale. You can see her but first, I have a few questions."

"Your letter said my wife was being detained for obstruction of justice. I tried to reach you by phone, but all I got was a recording."

"Sara said you'd come."

"Of course." Sam was losing patience. "Why didn't you let her call or pay a fine? Three days is a long time for a woman to be missing. I contacted the Highway Patrol two days ago."

"Sorry for your inconvenience," Layton said apologetically. "Way out here phone service tends to be a crap shoot. I'll straighten it out with the Patrol." He laid the letter on the thick-necked officer's desk. Sam noticed the deputy, or whatever he was, had been looking at a *Hustler* magazine. "Now about those questions."

"What questions?"

"Would you like to have a seat, Mr. Bingham?" Layton said.

"I'd like to see my wife."

"Sure you would. But first, why would you let her drive across the desert alone? Lot's of things can happen to a woman traveling alone."

Sam sighed and shrugged his shoulders. "She had a business appointment. I'm sure she told you that."

"Yes, I guess she did mention that."

"You haven't told me why she's being detained."

"Do you believe in eternal life?" Layton asked.

Sam looked at the sheriff, then at the other man and shuddered. Their expressions reflected anticipated humor awaiting a punch line.

"I think I'll make a phone call." Sam took his cell phone from the clip on his belt and started to dial.

Layton stood next to Sam before he could react. He grabbed Sam's phone and tossed it to the seated officer who plucked it easily from the air. The officer grinned at his accomplishment and shoved the cell phone inside his desk.

Fear gripped Sam like a blow to the chest. He could smell the dried sweat in the creases of Layton's uniform and his onion-laden breath against his cheek. "Now, wait a minute ..." Sam stuttered while horrible images assailed him. *What if two prisoners had broken out and killed the real sheriff and deputy? What if two lunatics had escaped from an asylum, tortured and killed Sara? What if. . ?*

"Answer my question and we'll get this business over with," Layton said, taking a step back. "Do you or don't you believe in life after death? Do you believe you'll be with your loved ones?"

What have they done to her? Sam's fear curdled his stomach, making him feel ill. "I don't know. Maybe."

"That's a pretty piss-poor response," Layton breathed, "but I guess it'll do." He patted Sam on the shoulder. "Since you cared enough about your wife to come for her, it'd be a shame to keep you apart any longer."

Layton turned and started toward the rear door. Sam momentarily considered reaching for the pistol in Layton's holster but the man behind the desk had shown he was quicker than he looked.

"If anything has happened to Sara or happens to me, the Highway Patrol knows about this place," Sam said with a touch of bravado.

"Oh really," Layton said, turning and raising his eyebrows. "That's not surprising seeing as how the Patrol for this part of the state is my cousin. He and I and Deputy Dog here have a lot in common." Layton continued toward the door while talking to Sam. "Don't go getting yourself all worked up, Mr. Bingham. We're just funnin' ya. Gets pretty boring way out here in the sticks. Lots of people come through, but not many single women. It's dangerous on these long stretches through the middle of nowhere but we've taken good care of Sara."

Sam looked past Layton and the deputy at the door in back … where the cells must be.

"You can see her, but last time I checked, she was having *a siesta*, so wake her slowly. She's been pretty jumpy."

"How about my phone?"

"Greg, let Mr. Bingham have his phone and wife's personals when we come out."

Layton opened the backdoor, which featured a square of wire glass. "You coming?" he asked Sam.

Sam followed the sheriff into the connecting room. It was dark. He could only make out the bars on the few cells.

"Can you turn on a light?" Sam asked.

"We've got a full house today. Our customers are more tolerable in the dark." Layton walked to the first cell and put the key in the lock.

"Then bring Sara out," Sam demanded.

"Who's running this place?" Layton said jovially. "She's probably asleep. I'll stand here with the door open so you'll feel safe."

"I'm not going in there. I can't see past the bars."

"All right, ya big baby," Layton teased and stepped into the darkened chamber.

As Sam's eyes adjusted, he could see a shape on a small bed covered with a rough blanket.

"Mrs. Bingham, your husband's here," Layton said softly. "Mrs. Bingham, time to rise and shine." He grasped the shadowy figure and sat her upright on the mattress.

A dim, dusty glow from the office shone through the bars onto the woman. Sam could make out the oval of a face surrounded by dishwater blond hair.

It was Sara. He could see she was awake and smiling slightly. "Sara," he called.

"It's time to go, Sara," Layton said, standing up.

"What's wrong with her?" Sam asked, his anxiety pouring out through his words.

"Oh, she'll be fine. She's smiling and waiting for you," Layton said cheerfully, his features masked in the dark haze within the chamber. "Waiting for you to die."

Sam's shoulder blades were jolted as the deputy shoved him from behind into the cubicle. Layton quickly sidestepped Sam and rushed out of the small space, locking the cell door behind him.

Sam rushed the bars. He reached through them, his hands becoming claws, trying to get to the sheriff and his deputy.

"Sara's going to be very good to us," Layton said as a high-pitched giggle erupted from the deputy. "You can have her for a little while. That's only fair. Then, you get to join the other husbands and boyfriends out in the cactus and sagebrush. But take heart. Since you're a believer, sort of, you've got eternity to be together, later on, when were done with your pretty wife."

Layton began to laugh, a small laugh at first, then rumbling into a roar that echoed through the room of cells. Sam put his hands over his ears trying to shut himself away from the mocking sound of a man enjoying his victory, a man no longer concerned about disturbing the supposed tenants in the other cells.

The laughter faded as Layton's persona turned somber. "We'll give you and Sara some privacy. Make the most of it, Mr. Bingham."

The door between the cells and the office closed with a sickening click of finality. Light shone through the door's small square of glass. It illuminated Sara's face. She smiled pleasantly at Sam.

He cautiously approached and sat next to her on the bed. "Sara, are you all right?"

Was she in some kind of trance? The dark woolen blanket draped her neck and shoulders. Sam pulled her to him and placed his head next to her silken hair. "Sara," he whispered. He put his hand between her shoulder blades and felt something on her back. Something course and alien. He ran his hand down her bare spine.

Sam gasped and backed away. A silent scream rose in his throat. The blanket slipped off her shoulders and fell onto her lap. She was naked. The outlines of her breasts were familiar and provocative. But the line on her back … a seam with stitches …

Suddenly, the room lit up with the force of a thousand watts from overhead florescent tubes and Sam saw his wife clearly. Her smile was almost natural except for tiny stitches in the corners of her mouth. Her eyes were bright but the wrong color. They were made of glass. And the seam down her backbone … Her skin had been sliced open and sewn back together.

"Christ She's stuffed Holy God " Sam flew from the bed and cringed against the far wall of the cell. He didn't realize he was screaming. He lunged at the bars, using all his energy to tear his way through them somehow.

There was a knock on the door that pounded into Sam's psyche like a sledgehammer against the outside of a crypt. Sam saw Layton's hideous face against the square of glass. His finger pointed to the right, inviting Sam to look in the adjacent cell.

Sam didn't want to look but he had to, the haunted act of a

man going insane. In the other cell were the bodies of a half-dozen naked women, life-sized Barbie Dolls, but with one notable difference. The bodies had been manipulated into grotesque erotic positions, human mannequins frozen into various *Hustler* poses.

The sheriff reentered the cellblock. "Did a good job on Sara, don't you think?" he smiled. "I'm not only the law for two hundred miles; I'm also a damn good taxidermist. Not quite finished with her though. We tried to find out what she liked best. Any suggestions, Sam?"

Sam made forlorn grunting noises at Layton, unable to form words; his saliva had dried up like dust.

"You're probably wondering why I bothered to write a letter. It's important to remove the *pater familious* and frankly, we get such a kick seeing the reactions when men reunite with their sweeties—how different all of you act. Like I said, it gets kinda slow around here."

Layton looked at Sam curiously. "I guess the cat's got your tongue. Don't worry about Sara. Greg and I are going to keep her nice and pliable for a long time, but I'm afraid your time is up."

Sam backed to the rear of the cell and looked one last time at what was left of his wife. Sara's corpse smiled its lifeless smile. Then, it slowly tilted and collapsed on its side with a thud. One blue glass eye popped out of its black socket and bounced across the cement floor toward Sam.

His mouth opened to scream again. Nothing came out but dry air followed by thick blood. He hadn't heard the sound of the gun and barely felt the bullet's sting.

"Remember, Sara is waiting for you just over the rainbow," Layton was saying. "Bet you'll think twice about crossing the desert alone in your next life."

"Love and marriage, love and marriage, go together like a horse and carriage." What was Old Blue Eyes drinking when he sang that one? Wedded bliss? I don't think so. Not for him or for the lovely couple in this next story.

Cottage For Sale

Ain't misbehavin', savin' my love for you, Redbone crooned from the CD player. His deep baritone voice wafted from the living room into the kitchen of the cottage Frank and his wife, Cyndi, had purchased only a short time ago. Redbone was her favorite balladeer since they had moved in, especially on sluggish, languid days devoted to house chores and yard work.

Frank came in the house through the back. He drank a glass of water at the kitchen sink and dabbed his sweaty forehead with a paper towel. He faintly heard Cyndi's voice between Redbone's warbles. She was on the bedroom phone again. He knew she was not talking to one of her girlfriends. The chatter was not light and airy, nor sprinkled with laughter. It was sober, conspiratorial.

He picked up the kitchen phone ever so carefully, put his hand over the speaker … and listened.

"I will call about ten o'clock," a man's voice said.

"Yes," Cyndi responded with a rush of air Frank could almost feel through the receiver.

"It will go fine, don't worry."

"What if he doesn't come out?"

"He will. We've been over and over this. Just make sure you answer the phone."

"All right. I love you."

"You too."

The disconnection sounded like a gunshot. Something broke inside Frank. His mind raced. He unexpectedly understood why Cyndi had been acting so strangely and going out with her girlfriends so much of late.

He returned the phone to its cradle, quickly walked out of the cottage's kitchen door, and around to the front yard where she would expect him to be, clipping away at the evergreens along the driveway.

So there is another man in her life after all, he brooded, *even though we just moved into the cottage that's supposed to be our love nest. The phone will ring and I'm supposed to go outside to face what? A pistol? A garrote? Could she actually want me dead?*

He should have known it would end this way with Cyndi. Their differences were destined to unleash a powerful clash between them. She was down right flamboyant compared to his rather reserved disposition, and since the move, she had been especially vibrant but at the same time, distracted. Oh, she had put on a marvelous act of being the dutiful housewife as part of her curriculum vitae, but sometimes being too obliging can be a clue to something hidden.

He could think of only one thing worse than finding a wife in *flagrante delicto* with another man, and that would be when the liaison involved the removal of said husband. Their little gambit might have succeeded if not for their carelessness with their conversation. But Frank knew the voice on the phone might not be careless again considering the intended prize was a juicy female with a newly acquired, substantial bank account.

Frank chopped at the hedge as if cutting off the limbs of this suspected interloper. He remembered the way it had been with his first wife. When he could not stand her a moment longer, he killed her with kindness until she had had enough. Was that what Cyndi had been doing? Killing with kindness? Acceptable. Killing with a weapon? Was she willing to go that far?

He wondered if he could possibly have misinterpreted the overheard conversation in any way, but decided the "I love you" was the clincher. What would happen if he told Cyndi he knew about her plan and she was free to go? Would she walk away without benefit of the house or his estate? Doubtful. She and her boyfriend would quickly form a new plan.

Frank heard the front door of their restored gingerbread cottage open. He paused as Cyndi waltzed across their front yard to join him. He was struck by the redness of her cheeks, the sparkle in her eyes, perhaps even a touch of embarrassment behind a smile that hid treachery.

"Get caught up in your music?" Frank asked her.

"No, darling. A call from the cleaners interrupted what I was doing. Thought I'd trot out and see if I could fix you some iced tea or make you a drink. Your arms must be getting tired?"

He chopped the head off another green branch then held the scissor blades down at his side. Now he could see beyond her gloss and straight through to her false heart. "Tea would be good."

"Okey dokey," she responded with the familiar curve of her lips that had first attracted him.

"What do you think of the hedge?" Frank asked.

"Oh, it looks fine, of course," she answered without really looking. "Things always look fine when you work on them. You coming in or shall I bring it out here?"

"No. I'll come in. I'm ready for a break." He followed her up the incline to the rear of the cottage. Her hips swayed to the music he imagined still played inside the house. It was no wonder other men found Cyndi attractive. She still had her figure and was full of life, a life that called for more than financial security. He supposed he had been foolish to corral this high-spirited woman into a serene life of ladies luncheons and backyard cocktails. And now, she was talking to some secret lover planning his demise. There could be no other explanation for the words he had overheard.

That evening, Cyndi prepared a marvelous beef tenderloin complete with chocolate mousse and a spot of brandy. *Last meal of a condemned man*, Jack mused throughout the proceedings. He tried to perform as if it were business as usual, and hoped he would not react abnormally when the telephone sounded the alarm.

It rang at precisely nine o'clock. Frank managed to stay calm for he had devised a plan of his own. "You want to get that dear?" he called to Cyndi from his study, sensing the relief that undoubtedly painted her face with the knowledge that there would be no race for the phone.

Frank heard her mumble a few nondescript words before hanging up. She walked into his sanctuary and faced him in the doorway, arms akimbo, as if working up the courage to turn her deceit into action.

"Frank," she said formally. "That was a call from one of our neighbors. He was driving past the house and saw a man lurking about in our front yard. He thought you would want to have a look?"

Is this the best they can do?, Frank thought. "A man lurking about?" he responded. "I should call the police." He watched Cyndi's face for a trace of concern or disappointment, but he saw neither.

"Whatever you think," she said, unruffled. "But it scares me. Couldn't you just check?" She did not seem anxious, only curious as to what he would do.

A cool one, this deceiving wench, Frank reflected. "I'll just take a peek out the window before I call them."

He peered through the living room curtains and then pulled away thinking his possible executioner might settle for a clear shot through the sheet of glass. He looked at Cyndi who rubbed one hand against the other, like someone in anticipation of an event.

"Don't see anything. Which neighbor called?"

The first chink in Cyndi's armor revealed itself. "I … I don't know really."

"The number should be on the handset," he offered.

"Oh, for Christ's sake, Frank. Why don't you just go out and see?" Now she was perturbed, anxious for him to meet his demise. "You want me to come out with you?," she added, a bit of condescension carving the corners of her infamous mouth.

Frank took a moment to speculate on what those pouting lips had been up to of late. He picked up the phone and was not surprised to see "NO DATA" in tiny green lines on the message screen. "Coming with me won't be necessary," he told Cyndi and headed for the back door.

If he did not fall into Cyndi and her lover's trap, he knew they would try something else at a later time, but why should he beat around the bush. If they wanted to do him in, why should he prolong the charade?

"Where are you going?" The sound of her apprehensive voice trailed off as Frank hurriedly closed the door behind him and picked up the hedge clippers he had left by the back door. He did not own a gun, but he felt sure these freshly sharpened blades should prove adequate if he could get close enough. He only needed to get around the house before Cyndi decided it prudent to wave her accomplice away.

Hustling past the side of the cottage, he saw a dark figure lurking behind the largest tree in the yard not far from the front porch. The plan Frank had worked out that afternoon would work fine if he could just get close enough to this lothario without being detected.

He crept along the well-tended lawn toward his would-be assassin. The sound of the metal blades rubbing against each other as they separated was just enough noise to make the man turn around.

Frank struck quickly, thrusting the blades forward, catching the man's neck in a vice. He crunched the handles together as far as his strength would allow them to go. Severing a head was more difficult than the movies would have you believe.

The man let out a small yip and blood spurted in two directions. Frank's arms did not possess the torque to decapitate the man, but the blades were in deep enough to send his victim to the ground without further complaint. He bled out quickly.

Frank felt a sudden revulsion for his actions, but there was no time to pity his victim, himself or his faithless wife. He searched the surrounding area and the dying man's pockets for a weapon … a gun, a knife, a rope … anything. But there was none. Could he have been wrong? No. The stranger had planned to choke him to death. Of course. If their plan was interrupted in some way, his wife's lover would not have wanted to be caught with a weapon? That had to be the answer.

Frank looked into the wide-open, unbelieving eyes of the man on his lawn that convulsed once then took his final gasp of life. *Where had Cyndi met this man?* Frank wondered. A luncheon? At a charity event or cocktail party? He attempted to sweep these irrelevant questions away and proceed with what needed to be done.

In the absence of a weapon, Frank realized he would need a new setup for the cops. Sweat beads again popped from his forehead. He quickly ran to the storage shed next to the garage and found a nice sized length of pipe. He left the shed's door ajar and wiped his own prints from the pipe before placing it in his supposed attacker's hand.

He hurriedly walked toward the front porch. Once the police

investigation ended and a relationship between the man he had killed and Cyndi was revealed, he would demand a divorce and hope to pick up the pieces of his life if the police would see it the way he hoped, as manslaughter two. He would have to play the game of being shocked that his wife could have planned such a thing, of course, but he would do what was necessary to make her pay for such treachery.

Cyndi opened the door. As Frank approached, he saw something shiny in her hand; a small caliber pistol. He stopped in his tracks and said the only words he could think of on short notice. "What's that for?"

He should have known the answer, should have thought about her motives more closely. Maybe she thought something might go wrong too. *Would she settle for the money instead of the man? Could that be it?*

Without a word, Cyndi squeezed off a single shot that entered Frank's chest exploding his heart. He fell to the ground with little more than a whimper, with no more fanfare than his victim he had left sprawled beneath the large elm tree in the cottage's front yard. He was gone before his mind could sort out the answers he would have liked.

Cyndi worked fast on her back-up plan in the event a nosy neighbor heard the single blast. She dragged Frank's body near the first, idly wondering if he had been surprised to be greeted with a bullet instead of a kiss. She saw what her husband's handiwork had done to Joe, marveled at his apparent knowledge of the scheme, and his gutsy choice of weapons to take on whatever had been waiting. She tilted her head curiously at the sight of her lover, his head nearly separated from his body. But she had no time to dwell on disquieting facts as she replaced the pipe with the gun in her former lover's hand.

She returned to her living room and dialed 911. "There's been a shooting on Blueberry Lane," she said excitedly into the phone.

"1300 Blueberry Lane. My husband and another man. My husband isn't breathing. Please hurry." She threw in a few whimpering sounds for good measure before hanging up.

Cyndi slid into the easy chair next to the phone and waited, knowing what lay ahead. She had moved Frank quickly before blood pooled on the lawn where he fell and she had seen enough TV to know there would most likely be some business about angle of the bullet and direction of the murder weapons, not to mention the implications between she and the second victim. They had been careful, but still ... It was a chance she had been willing to take.

"Had she set up one or both of the victims,?" she would be asked She had thought about what tact to follow depending on the result of the confrontation between the two men. She knew if one of the men took care of the other, she would have to finish it with her little revolver she had been instructed to purchase only a few days earlier.

"Yes, it is worth it," she breathed.

The phone rang. Cyndi picked it up and listened without speaking.

"You have done it, my darling," a deep yet soft, gentile voice said to her.

"Yes. Just as you wanted. Now it belongs to just the two of us."

"Yes, Cynthia. Yes. Just the two of us."

"When will you come to me? Please don't keep me waiting any longer. Only I can see and hear you. Please come now before the police arrive. Oh please, Daniel."

"There is only one way, my sweet. I am bound to the cottage I built. I can't leave. You know that."

"You'll wait here then while I'm questioned? And then when I return—"

"There is a better way—a way in which they cannot separate

us. Use the pistol one more time, my precious. Retrieve your gun. It doesn't matter how it looks now. We will possess the house together, for always, just you and I."

"But I thought … you said …"

"I said we needed to remove those two fools before we could be joined, but you must join me now if I am to be more than a voice and the shadow of an image to you. You must come over. Do it now before the authorities come and take you away. They may not believe your story. They may not let you return to be at my side. You must act now, quickly, painlessly."

"Did you know from the start that I must do this to be with you?" Her clever, curved lip trembled.

"Dear Cynthia. You are the only one for me, and I for you." The voice on the phone grew fainter, more distant. "It is the only way to be sure we will not be separated. For eternity, Cynthia. You must trust me. Do it now."

Cyndi put the phone down and walked to the CD player. She programmed it to play her favorite Redbone tune, *Ain't Misbehavin'*.

＊＊＊

Investigators did little more than scratch their heads and wonder how this macabre love/hate triangle managed to end in such a bewildering state. What was certain was the fact that this had not been the only tragedy in the beautiful cottage.

First, the wife of Daniel Bloom, the builder, had murdered him for philandering decades earlier. Following that, a family lost their young child under suspicious circumstances and moved away, and now this grisly episode. Normally, Detective Phipps was not a superstitious man, but in this instance, he believed a "Buyer Beware" notice should be placed alongside the placard that read "Cottage for Sale."

And now for the novella. For this story, you can't pick up your food at the drive-thru window. You must come inside and stay awhile, for the night, at least. Happy eating and reading, and I hope at the end, you will have enjoyed the journey.

Descent Into Darkness

CHAPTER 1

What gives worth to a life? Is it acts of goodwill or righteous living? I'm afraid I fall short if that's the measuring stick. Or, is it the pursuit of our hopes and dreams whether real or imagined? Moreover, where does awareness leave off and madness begin? These questions torment me as I seek my path into the future, hungering for the truth of what really happened.

In the beginning, I only saw little things from the corner of my eye—a glimpse of something here or there, slight movement in an adjoining room. Upon investigation, everything appeared untouched. Normal.

Later, my sanctuary lost its subtlety. Inanimate objects brazenly found new homes around the house. I would've bet my ass either progressing age or, God forbid, Alzheimer's, was the culprit. Could I be sliding into senility like a dinosaur into a tar pit? Hell, I was only fifty-five. I should have lots of healthy years left.

What a kick in the butt if my mind turned to cottage cheese so soon after losing my wife.

Is there no sadder transfer than desire given over to pity? I watched Carol wither and die. I was at her bedside when her eyelids closed for the last time and remember how alone I felt as they lowered her box into the ground.

My son, Ryan, was off at the state university, and I spent many nights touching Carol's place in bed, wondering how I'd manage without her; how people managed to watch those they care for fade from their lives.

After the initial shock, I handled the guilt and remorse phases pretty well, but twenty-five years of marriage still left a load of *what if's*, and *why didn't I's* to sort out. They sometimes spun around in my head like an old, scratchy 33 1/3 LP.

A sadness lingered, however. I supposed it happens to all men in their mid-fifties. A time when one looks back on things he regrets or wishes he had done differently.

Had I done right by my wife while she was here? Had she picked the right man to share her shortened life with? Had I picked the right woman? These were questions that had crossed my mind over the last few months. And sometimes it seemed like there was an attempt from somewhere to provide answers—a message from spirits that passed in and out of unfocused dreams, their names lost to the past.

At any rate, it was time to do something for myself. Eleven months after Carol's passing, I decided I'd pushed bureaucratic pencils around long enough, and took an early retirement. Having slain the job-dragon, I began to think of the future rather than the past. Without a female waiting in the wings or a social group to fill the void, I pondered my new bachelor status.

I thought of calling old acquaintances from years past. Maybe I'd climb into my old black Jag and drive a few hundred miles to pester them. I could return to my hometown to see if the houses where I'd spent a portion of my gangly youth still existed, and if they harbored the same residents. I could still remember parlors where I used to sit, my neck itching from a fresh haircut, waiting for some ingénue to descend a stairway so I could take her to a high school dance. It might be a kick to find out what happened to some of them.

In the end, I never made the calls or took the trips. These people had their own lives going. I didn't want to be the widowed intruder. The time had come to connect with simple pleasures: Taking long walks with my trusty Nikon, and setting up a darkroom to play in. If that bored me, I could always work a few hours buying and selling ball cards at the neighborhood nostalgia shop.

Actually, I'd always been drawn to the image of a man alone. The Raymond Chandler character who had a single room apartment, a bottle of cheap hooch, an occasional dame, and a personal sense of justice. This could be me, but with a comfortable home, a well-stocked bar, the hope of getting laid occasionally, and my own set of screaming liberal views by which to live. Modest ambitions, I thought.

But then, stuff started happening. The plants moved. Large silk ones scattered through my sun porch and living room. I mean the fucking philodendrons changed places with the ferns. I'm pretty compulsive. When I get something the way I want it, I'm not likely to change it. Some kind of delayed stress syndrome perhaps, either from Carol's passing, or a hallucinatory reaction from having this sudden free time. I kept worrying about Alzheimer's although I hadn't a clue as to what actually happens with diseases of aging.

I wasn't frightened so much as puzzled. Often, Carol and I had watched movies where things went bump in the night. Mystery movies were fun and Carol had a sixth sense about whodone-it. But we especially enjoyed *spookers*, relishing in the horrible performances and ridiculous plot twists. In real life, we would've been checking in at a Holiday Inn the first time a house moaned, or an object flew across a room, we thought.

So what to do when you come home and some force has seen fit to redecorate? I soon discovered that you *don't* go to the Holiday Inn. Too gutless. Just like in the movies, you stay and try to figure it out, or refuse to acknowledge what's happened.

What I told my house was, "Listen. I've never been in therapy and I don't feel like going through any psychobabble at this late date. So please house, don't rearrange any more shit. I'll cut down on the late night TV super gore if you'll quit fucking with me."

It seemed to work for a while. But then, something happened that scared the happy-crappy right out of me. It was damned subtle though. Some of my desktop mementos changed places.

I used to prefer that Carol dust around my gems rather than move them. Imagine the effect on someone as compulsive as I when my life long treasures started to slow tango during the night. Discovering these subtle changes proved more horrific than if they'd been tossed in a corner willy-nilly.

One evening while seated at my desk, I looked at a small hand-carved wooden totem I'd purchased in Canada. My blood felt frozen in my veins when I saw that the creatures had reconfigured themselves. The hawk at the top had repositioned himself to the bottom, supporting the frog and the serpent.

I sat there trembling. I closed my eyes tightly and counted to ten. When I reopened them the figures had returned to their proper order, but I knew what I had seen.

Then I found something that wouldn't change back. The railroad cars on my Lionel train, lovingly preserved since childhood and preciously guarded through my son's youth, had not only changed positions, but also switched logos and decals. I closed my eyes again and counted to fifty this time, until my eyes watered. The new combinations still existed.

Standard poltergeist stuff? Maybe so, but at least I'd ruled out Alzheimer's. It struck me that the preservation of my possessions was the least real thing in my life. I'd better have something more tangible than treasured "things."

Maybe all I needed was more fresh air. A lot more. Plenty of that in my neighborhood near the Mile High City. And if I moseyed home one day and the light bulbs had changed from soft white to disco blue, it would be time for a brain scan before I lost the nerve to go home altogether.

In the days that followed, I spent considerable time on excursions to the foothills, shooting uninspired rolls of black and white film and thinking about my house. Some creepy shit had been going on that could challenge the sensibility of anyone. Yet I remained Ty Pierson of Golden, Colorado, college grad, recently retired, with a grown son, a dead wife and a reasonable amount of my mind intact. There had to be reasonable explanations somewhere.

Once reassured, I went home, mixed a drink, and cautiously looked around for anything new and exciting in my decorative scheme. I didn't look *too* hard, mind you. Didn't go out of my way. Just a casual glance here or there while going through my nightly routine of dinner, reading or TV, and going through photo prints.

The light bulbs never changed colors. But, to my amazement, under the red glow of the darkroom bulb, my photos changed. "Now, how bout this shit " I said the way my friend, Butch would have said it.

Actually, the pictures began to improve. Framing mundane photography hadn't surprised me, considering all that occupied my mind during those times. The compositions I'd arranged through the lens were slightly off from the prints coming off the developer, but they were better for it. My kooky mind was doing something positive. The contrasts were richer.

I saw rolling clouds that hadn't been there while shooting. The textures, the subtlety of light and shadow were fantastic. I just wondered where it all had been when I had focused and shot. Some of these prints Ansel Adams might have approved of, by God.

"What the fuck is happening now? Am I just totally nuts?" I asked the walls. If I were a hard-drinking man, I'd start looking for bats on the walls instead of bats in the belfry. What finally sent me directly to the liquor cabinet for straight bourbon, no water—that's what fish make love in—were two photographs I'd taken in the foothills.

They revealed a young woman smiling, ever so slightly, caught in profile, partially hidden behind a huge boulder. No one had been in these photographs when I shot them. If I were to choose some flight of fancy, I'd have expected to see a naked water sprite or Tinkerbell flitting from one print to another. The female image in my photos merely leaned against a boulder, her head slightly turned to one side, revealing a cheekbone, black close-cropped hair, and long fingers resting on one visible thigh. There was no misty quality to her image. She wore a soft sweater and faded jeans. A pretty girl. Very pretty, and young enough to be my daughter.

This convinced me that my reality was definitely askew. The time had come for a second opinion.

CHAPTER 2

"How the hell are you, Ty-man?" Butch asked while mixing some concoction behind the bar of his modest art deco apartment. "You look tired and wired at the same time. Drinking lots of prune juice or what? No? Then maybe you should try what I'm having. I recommend one of these strong, nasty ones."

I took his advice and accepted a strong, nasty one.

Leonard (Butch) Washington was a sharp dude. I liked him a lot. There hadn't been many guys from work I'd socialized with, but Butch and I hit it off from the get-go. We'd shared a few drinks and seen a few ballgames over the years. He'd not only been the only black guy in my section, but also the only cool guy as far as I was concerned. After all, he'd been willing to hang out with me.

"How the hell is that boy of yours?" His words danced from his mouth like the brass section of a swing band. "He gettin' laid up at school?" His wide grin was disarming.

I had to smile back. "Guess he's doing fine. Can't drag him down much anymore for even a weekend."

"Hey man, be glad he's not on your doorstep every other week with his palm out. My Joseph always was. I think his momma use to send him off with two or three days worth of food."

"I'm glad he's having a good time. I think he misses his mom more when he's home. Anyway, why come home to hang around with a single pop who qualifies for the Sears Mature Lifestyle Discount Card?"

"Is this self-pity I'm hearing? If so, it don't look good on you, man. Hey, maybe I should be asking if *you* are gettin' laid instead?" he offered as we made our way to his overstuffed, incredibly comfortable couch.

"No such luck," I answered, settling in. "But a female is part of what I want your opinion on."

"I say do it, man. Whether she walks or only crawls. You got it coming." His eyes watched me as he took a healthy swallow of his nasty one.

"Butch, what I want to tell you is a ghost story, I guess." I hesitated and thought about how to approach the subject, and what might be gained by relating the events of the past few weeks. But a comfort zone existed with Butch, and that was where I needed to be.

"This might be good," Butch exclaimed while I was still thinking about how to put it together. "Maybe I should bring the jug over here."

When he returned, he wore an amiable "I'm listening" look. I told my tale with as few embellishments as possible. I regurgitated the behavioral highlights of objects and photos, which included the mystery woman leaning on the rocks. Butch listened attentively till I finished.

He took a long, slow drink. "My buddy's dad has prostate cancer. Then, they cut it out and he was fine for a time. Then, his PSA started to climb again like a monkey on a tree. They had to castrate his ass this time. But, the Big C just kept coming back, other places, you know." Butch sighed and took another measured sip. "So now, the poor bastard's going down for the third and final time. Makes you think, huh?"

"Kind of puts my concerns in perspective, I guess."

"Damn right. I'm not trying to make light of whatever you're going through. I still say you need to get laid, but I don't think you need a shrink. You're straight, man. You ain't nuts. If there's something going on in your head, I think someone or something is putting it there. Tell you what. I'm going to give Doris a call tomorrow. Her sister knows about this lady called Mama Shari." Butch studied my sarcastic smile. "Hold on now. Just hear me out. One night she was telling Doris and me about how this Mama Shari can see shit and do the aura thing on you."

"Sounds like Miss Cleo. I don't think—"

"No, no, wait a minute. Her sister went to see Mama because of some bad shit that was happening in her life. Anyway, Mama figured out that a girlfriend of hers had been affecting her thought process in some way. Hypnosis or something."

I couldn't keep the corners of my mouth from curling up at Butch's story. "I didn't know you bought into this kind of stuff?"

"Hey, I'm not talking about some card reader. She is an educated woman, or so I was told. I believe in a little bit of everything, man. You've been around long enough to have experienced a little magic dust now and then, haven't you?"

I tried not to sound too skeptical. "I've had my share of magical moments. Like when Ryan discovered something new about life. Or when I discovered something new about women in the high school parking lot. But, it sounds like some kind of voodoo bullshit. She probably practices somewhere Whitey's not allowed."

Butch straightened his arm and good-naturedly pointed a finger and his cocktail glass at me. "Man, you've been watching too many movies about a bunch of natives beating on drums in the Caribbean."

"You're probably right about that," I said laughing. "But, I'm not sure I'm ready for this approach. I'll think it over."

"No sweat then," Butch replied. "But think about it, and know that I'm always here for you."

He offered me another nasty one before I left. I declined and patted him on the back, appreciative of his listening and his friendship. We discussed the latest failures of Denver's sports franchises while walking to the door.

As we shook hands, I found myself saying, "What the hell. Give your ex a call. Nothing ventured, nothing gained. Just so she doesn't paint my ass and put a dead chicken on it. I'd still take that over a shrink's couch."

"You don't need a couch. You're too damn passive to be a loony. I'll call you when I get the info. I have to pick the right time to ask Doris for anything. Know what I'm saying?"

I nodded.

"Just stay loose, T P. Everything's cool."

I thanked him again for listening and drove home. On the way, I thought about my rock girl. Funny how I considered her to be mine. If she was merely a figment of my imagination, I suppose she did belong to me. At the same time, I felt certain I'd see her again.

Something in my life was changing. It felt as if I were being sucked into a melodrama toward some eventual conclusion beyond my control. Each event I'd experienced was some signpost marking the way through the twilight zone toward an epiphany or perhaps, a cataclysm. If a reason or purpose existed, it would become clear as it played out. At least, that's what I hoped.

It felt like the beginning of a movie. All I needed was a music sound track. Strangely, this provided a sense of calm. Maybe insanity is a great adventure, the same way dreams are.

CHAPTER 3

She did exist, this pretty girl.

A week after visiting Butch, I found myself in downtown Golden on a beautiful, unseasonably warm April day. This time I wasn't seeing her in the dark room on a sheet of paper, nor did I have her to myself. She sat in a public place.

While I sat in an ice cream joint on Washington Street eating lime sherbet in a cone, I saw her sitting three tables away having coffee and reading a textbook. I knew this encounter was inevitable, but her reality still jolted me. No ghost. No mirage. Flesh and blood.

I wondered what would happen if I didn't approach her. Would she approach me? Were the events yet to unfold so irreversible that if I got up and walked off, I would see her in the park, or at the mall, and be compelled to make contact?

This moment was pivotal in my life. Had I known the consequences, I can only speculate if I would've had the willpower to act differently.

I finished my cone, got up, and walked to her table. She stopped reading and raised her eyes to meet mine.

"I'm sorry," I stammered, "but I believe I know you." I stared dumbly at her, not thinking of anything to add.

"You think so, huh?" She said it with a friendly smile that revealed perfect teeth to compliment her green eyes.

I hadn't expected such a warm reception. I plunged on. "Yes. You're my rock lady."

She laughed, her gaze never leaving mine. "Your rock lady? I've been called some funny things before, but never that."

Her brilliant eyes were riveting. The greenest eyes I'd ever seen, offering an ocean of desire I could only dream of. Of course, I fell in love instantly.

"Can I sit down for a minute? I'm dying to tell you about the rocks, which I hope aren't just in my head."

Tilting her head as if observing some new curiosity, she seemed to be thinking it over, then glanced at her watch. "I have a class in a little while. You can walk with me to my car if you like."

"Yes, sure. That'd be great."

We walked toward a park at the foot of Main Street. I wondered again what this encounter meant. Maybe it wasn't the girl in my pictures after all. Maybe I was just being a stupid middle-aged goose?

She clutched her book to her chest like a schoolgirl while we walked. "So what about me and your rocks?"

"You don't remember being my photo subject a week ago? In the foothills?" I said as casually as I could, matching my steps to hers.

She stopped, looked at me inquisitively, and then laughed heartily. It was almost the cackle of an older person, the only thing I'd noticed that detracted from her near perfection.

"I'm sorry," she said with a little gasp. "I've never been anyone's model. I go there to meditate occasionally. She looked away momentarily, and then back at me coquettishly. "And you photographed me? You devil."

A child lurks inside most men, alert to an opportunity to cast the drudgery of routine aside. Pushing ahead, feeling rakish, I told her, "I've never had a more pleasing subject, nor one I wanted to shoot again more desperately."

We strolled another block to the car. She unlocked her compact, tossed her book on the seat, and we talked for what seemed an eternity.

Her name was Michelle Devin, twenty-five years young and finishing a graduate program while working part-time. As we spoke, I felt a thread existed within her that had run through my life long ago. Something about her—a look more sensual than a touch, a tone more meaningful than words.

As I watched her, casually leaning there, smiling, and talking, she looked like a model out of an L.L. Bean catalog. She was a great deal closer to the age of my son than to mine, but a father figure was definitely not the image that toyed with my mind.

"I've got to scoot," she finally said.

Knowing I hadn't appeared to be listening and feeling foolish, I pulled myself together long enough to ask, "Would you consider meeting me for lunch so I could show you the pictures?"

She puzzled over the question. Now I was being mushy. Michelle was thirty years my junior.

She flashed another smile. "Sure, why not, Mr. Pierson. How about you give me your number and I'll call you. I have an awfully busy schedule between school and work."

"That'd be great," I said but my hopes plummeted. *She won't call.* First she found me to be a curiosity, now she's trying to gracefully escape. All these feelings of inevitability were just so much bunk.

I dashed off my number on a card. She took it and then offered her hand. I grasped it and shivered at her touch.

"Well, nice meeting you. I'll give you a call," she said brightly and climbed into her car.

"I'll polish off my portfolio along with your pictures," I said stupidly, shutting the door for her.

Off she went, out of my life I supposed. But if so, why these photos and these feelings? I had little choice but to wait and hope that I would hear from her. It gave me something to offset the dread of what my ghosts might be up to.

CHAPTER 4

That night I threw the latest issue of *Vanity Fair* on the rug next to my bed and sat up. I wasn't sleepy. The digital clock read 1:06. The caller ID read "4 NEW CALLS." I looked at my reflection in the antique, full-length mirror that stood on four dragon talons in the corner of the bedroom. I saw a naked, fifty-five-year-old man looking back at me.

I reached for my plastic cup that contained the watered-down remnants of a Pepsi and thought about what my life had become. There was ample time to ponder such a weighty issue, as I had not slept well any number of nights, for obvious reasons. Now, I waited, hoping this Michelle would call someday. Vowing to do something productive before another day passed, I promised myself to call Butch and invite him to a ball game.

The following day, the Rockies had an afternoon game. Once at the ballpark, Butch philosophized between sips of his beer. "Hey, maybe just a sniff of young stuff was all you needed to straighten your ass out."

"Maybe so," I agreed, wondering what I could have been thinking concerning Michelle. I hadn't been out with anyone the sunny side of forty-five in the last two years. Come to think of it, I hadn't been with anyone Michelle's age since the good old polyester seventies. If I had a lick of sense, I'd get Michelle right out of my head. It wouldn't do me any good now anyway.

"What happened with Mama Shari?" I asked Butch, hoping I wouldn't be sorry I brought it up.

"That option is still there. I checked it out, but thought I'd give you some time. See if your spooks stayed after you. If you want to dance to that tune, you can give her a call. Hell, I'll go with you."

"Think I'll cool it for now. No bumps in the night for a couple of weeks."

"That's a shame, man. I keep telling you some humpin' and bumpin' is what you need, no disrespect to Carol. Hey, hit the ball, fool " Butch yelled at the batter. "Man, I think I could still play with these bums."

✱✱✱

My phone rang at one the next morning. Through the cobwebs on my corneas, I checked the time, then caller ID. "Blocked." I picked up the receiver.

"Lo?"

"Mr. Pierson?"

Could it be? I was afraid to ask. "Yeah, this is Ty."

"You were sleeping, I guess. I'm sorry."

"No. That's okay."

"You've probably forgotten me."

Pause.

"This is Michelle Devin. We met in Golden a few weeks ago."

"Oh yeah. Sure, I remember," I said calmly, my heart pounding so hard I thought it might jump out of my mouth.

"I know it's late, but I was thinking of you and well … I have a problem I'd like to discuss. Do you have time to see me tomorrow? Well, later today actually."

"Uh … sure. When's good?"

"Tonight. After I'm off work."

"All right. Where can I meet you?"

"I'm not really much for going out late. Would you mind if I came to your house? I promise not to take too much of your time. Would that be okay?"

Would that be okay? Come and never leave would be okay. "Sure," I said. "If that works for you, it'll work for me."

"Around nine then. All I need is your address."

I didn't sleep much after hanging up thinking of a hundred reasons she might've called me. Not having just fallen off the turnip truck, I weighed the possibility that her *problem* would be one that was designed to take advantage of my obvious interest in her. *I won't be taken in by any sort of scam, rock girl or not.*

Finally, it was time to quit psychoanalyzing the situation and get my carcass out of the sack. I sat up and whipped my feet to the floor.

I gasped. Putting my hand to my mouth to stifle a scream, I jumped back against my pillows, trying to put distance between the object and myself. Standing not three measly feet away stood a three and a half foot antique stein from my study.

I looked around my bedroom to see if this piece was solo or if an army of marching ornaments had followed along. The French stein stood alone. Ironically, this particular piece took my thoughts away from Michelle and to Carol. It was one of my few treasures she really liked.

The huge ceramic piece has two figures, a cavalier and his lady, perched on the lid. They smiled benignly as they always had, and I could almost hear them say, "Hello asshole. What's new?" How could this twenty-pound stein have arrived at my bedside without sound or notice?

I just sat and stared for several moments, clutching my bed sheets. I knew, once and for all, that my world had gone bug-fuck crazy. I wondered if I should touch the stein, or if I should move it back. It seemed that things would move where they wanted to, either way.

Fighting the temptation to believe Michelle's call was connected to this *event*, I vowed two things: One was not to be afraid. If I was crazy, then I was crazy. Why worry? The second thing was to ask Butch for Mama Shari's number. Being certifiable would go down easier if someone attached some rationale to it all. Sometimes the illusion of sanity can work as well as sanity itself.

***

In spite of my confrontation with the Cavalier and his lady, that evening I sung in the shower, shaved carefully, sloshed mouthwash until my tongue was stinging, and plucked my favorite shirt from the closet. It had been a very long time since I'd devoted this much attention to my appearance. After a final inspection, I made a drink, put on a Nat King Cole tape and tried to sit casually at one end of my heavily stuffed sofa.

When the phone rang, something broke inside me. I just knew it was Michelle calling the evening off. To my surprise and delight, it was Ryan. He'd been in a minor fender bender on campus, rear-ended by a coed.

"It was her fault, but she's awfully cute and oh, so sorry," Ryan told me.

I reminded him not to be swayed by a fair damsel, ironic advice to give at this particular time. "If it's her fault, make sure her insurance pays."

"It'll be taken care of. You doing all right?"

The question now took on a whole new dimension since I had no frigging idea how I was. "Just dandy," I said, as usual. I thought about telling Ryan I was expecting female company, but decided it would either raise a bunch of ticklish questions or worse, he wouldn't care.

"Stay out of trouble and keep me posted on the car and girl." I hung up and prepared for my visitor by straightening the house a little—no major objects out of place including the wayward stein—and chilling some wine in case she drank.

Nine o'clock came and went, followed by ten o'clock, and no call. I'd discovered the second thing that bothered me about Michelle. But, maybe she had to work late and I had nothing but time.

At a quarter to eleven, I'd started to turn out the lights when I heard her knock. I took a quick glance in the bathroom mirror, not caring much for what I saw and wished, just for tonight, I could cast off the past twenty-five years. I proceeded to the door and peered through the peephole.

My overhead porch light cast a golden glow upon Michelle as she stood outside, expectantly. Her hair was longer, falling around her face, perfectly setting off her cocked head and impish smile. I opened my world to her.

"I'm so, so sorry, Mr. Pierson. Complications at work to add to everything else."

Determined not to utter, "No problem," I roguishly said, "Ten minutes more and I would've been naked and wet. Thank goodness you made it."

"Oh, I'm really sorry. If it's too late, I understand."

"Of course not," I said smiling. "No problem." Old habits die hard.

She came in. Wearing a short skirt and no jacket, I couldn't help but admire the shape of her legs as well as her décolletage. I felt a little lecherous, sort of like Christopher Walken's *The Continental* from an old *Saturday Night Live* show.

"Oh, Mr. Pierson, what a gorgeous house. It suits you."

"Yeah, I guess it does. *Complete with moveable objects.* "Would you like the nickel tour?"

"God, I'd love it, but it's so late, thanks to me."

"Tell you what. Let me get you something and we'll do a quickie tour. What can I offer you? I have tidbits and some *rose.*"

"You're so sweet. I grabbed a bite on the way. I wasn't about to come over with my belly flattened to my backbone. But I'd love some wine."

Fetching two glasses and a bottle, I poured and we took our first sips.

"This is so good. Don't tell me you have a wine cellar in this beautiful house as well?"

"No. Just your weekly liquor store special."

"Mr. Pierson, you do have excellent taste."

"Okay. We're going to get over this 'Mr. Pierson' stuff. I'm going to be bold and give you my official 'Welcome to my house' greeting."

She looked at me with either delight or curiosity. I couldn't tell which, but either would do. I put my arms around her and firmly hugged. "Welcome to my house," I said. "And from here on, it's Ty. All right?" I held her as long as I thought prudent without being too blatant. When we separated, I was relieved to see she was still smiling, enjoying this encounter.

"Yes sir. From now on it's Ty," she said, giving me a mock salute.

After a short tour, we settled in the living room with the wine bottle. I sat kitty-cornered from her.

Michelle kicked off her shoes, with my permission, and languished on my sofa. I could see the epistle written in stone:

Here lies a beautiful twenty-five year old woman with the face and body to make the angels weep, holding her second glass of wine, preparing to tell me her trials and tribulations. I froze this moment in time, having no right to expect it would get any better than this.

Then our journey began.

"Ty, could I stay with you tonight?" she asked, raising her eyebrows.

Almost choking on a mouthful of *rose*, I cleared my throat and tried to keep my cool.

"Why would you want to stay here? Are you in some kind of trouble?"

"Not trouble exactly. I have two problems. There's this guy. He's stalking me. He's a professional, yuppie guy who spotted me in the shop where I work. He came in often and was pretty nice. Well, he asked me out. I declined, but after that, he still came into the shop all sullen-like, I guess you'd say."

I poured myself another glass and drank in her story along with the wine.

"Then, I spotted him in my apartment parking lot, and knew he'd been following me. There's little I can do without any overt action on his part, but a girl was murdered on campus a year ago and that's enough to make me terribly frightened."

"Who wouldn't be," I said sympathetically. *And who wouldn't follow you*, I mused.

Secondly, she told me about her noisy roommate who liked to party. Michelle was afraid she wouldn't be able to complete her course work.

Then she popped the question. "I thought you might let me stay here for a while? Of course, I'll pay you rent."

I did have more room than I needed, but my question for her was, "Why me?"

"I felt so at ease when we met," she said. "There must be some connection between us. I meant to get in touch sooner, but have been so busy lately with work and school. Quite frankly, when I thought about a refuge, you immediately come to mind. I could sure stand being around someone who's mature for a change."

I assumed that her intentions were plutonic and, in spite of all the signals, I gathered my role was to be that of the mature figure. I was delighted to give her shelter. "I think we can work something out," I said, accepting her praise and letting it go at that, not about to analyze the situation by using common sense. Not this time.

We talked until quite late. She seemed so forthright, just a young girl in need of some stability. I tried to keep the subject off of myself, but she insisted on hearing about Carol, my son, and past relationships. She told me how brave I'd been and how she admired me. All this flattery, with two and a half bottles of wine consumed between us, would have been enough, but then I told her to take her pick of the guest rooms.

"I hope I don't embarrass you, but I'd rather sleep with you."

I stopped playing with my wine glass. My testicles tightened from want of her. "Are you absolutely sure about that?"

"Never more sure of anything since my return."

I moved next to her on the sofa and kissed her parted lips tenderly.

We kissed again, then fondled, and then we took the remaining wine into my bedroom.

Her lovemaking was intense. The feel of her erased twenty of my years, and she seemed as hungry as I for the closeness, as if their mightn't be another chance for our bodies to become one. I prayed that wouldn't be true as we drank and rejoiced in one another's pinnacle of passion.

✳✳✳

The next morning, Michelle lay with her head on my chest, her naked breasts against me. As her breathing rose and fell, I reviewed the events of the evening. A young woman had ravished me. We had ravished each other. What a wonderfully delicious night it had been. My manhood had returned with a force more suited to a hungry young man Michelle's age.

Consummation with this living, breathing piece of art had been satisfying, but no more so than admiring her from afar earlier in the evening. As corny as it may sound, watching this delicate creature sleeping softly next to me was the richest moment. It was truly a time to think, *Powers-that-be. If you're going to take me, take me now.*

I looked at my ceiling and noticed its rough texture. I thought how it contrasted with the silkiness of Michelle's skin. Everything seemed tactile, vibrant, and more alive.

When she awoke, she looked up and smiled with an expression that now seemed strangely familiar. "Hi guy."

"Hey, you."

She snuggled against the crack between my arm and chest.

"Ty?"

"Mmm?"

"What's it like for you?"

"What's what like?"

"I mean, how do I feel when you make love to me?"

I thought for a moment. This is where men often have to concoct a glorious tale of ethereal bliss beyond the physical pleasure they've enjoyed. But in this case, any words I could have strung together would ring hollow compared to the joy I had experienced in Michelle's arms.

"Baby, you're the greatest," I said.

She looked at me ... through me ... then pinched my cheek and laughed.

"Is that the best you can do? Quote Jackie Gleason?"

"I'm surprised you know who Jackie Gleason is."

"Mom knows that kind of stuff."

"Mom?"

"I'll tell you about her sometime."

I didn't care to hear about mother at the moment and reached for Michelle's thigh outlined beneath a sheet.

"Nope. That's it for you, mister," she said. "If you're not going to tell me romantic thoughts of lust, I might as well get a move on." Michelle crawled over me. "I need a shower. Do you mind?"

"*Mi casa es su casa.*"

"Want to join me."

I was tempted, but it almost seemed too much of a good thing. "I think I'll just lie here, relax, and think about last night a while longer."

She laughed, giving me a warm kiss, then dashed to the bathroom. I watched her walk away, her bare bottom swaying with each step. The words "voluptuous" and "juicy" came to mind. I'd almost forgotten how beautiful and erotic the movements of a young woman could be.

While she showered, I heard her humming happily, which pleased me. Then I heard that witch's cackle. Although disquieting, it was a small enough flaw, I decided, everything considered.

She emerged, wrapped in a towel and began to gather her clothes.

"What brought on your laughing fit?" I asked.

"You mean my ghoulish laugh? Not too attractive I know, but sometimes I just have to let go."

"So, what caused it this time?"

"I'll never tell," she said. "I can't talk to anyone about what I was thinking except my mother."

"Your mother? I guess it wasn't about us, then?"

"It most certainly *was* about us. I always said I'd tell my mother when I found the man of my dreams."

"Not me, surely."

"Ty," she said as she sat next to me. "You are a caring, tender, unique man. Your age means nothing to me. You're as vital as men half your age, and I think you proved it last night."

I brushed the hair away from her face.

"I only hope you don't think this is an act I'm pulling to get a place to stay?" she continued, looking into my eyes.

"I'm not sure I'd care if it was," I answered, trying to control my emotions.

"Well, it's not." With mock anger she stood, removed her towel and swatted me.

Lunging for her, she danced out of my reach and wiggled her finger at me.

"No, no. No more for you, young man. You had your chance at the shower. I've got to get myself together. I've got classes, you know."

"What about your stuff?"

"I can get everything I own in two suitcases. I'll bring them tonight, unless you've changed your mind."

"Yeah, right," I said, mockingly.

"I'll take that as a 'No.' You'll see me and my bags later," she said determinedly, getting dressed.

Wrapped in her discarded towel, I saw her to the door. How long had it been since I'd seen a woman off in this manner? That would take some serious thought.

I watched her saunter down the walkway and caught a glimpse of her thighs as she climbed into her little car. She was as strange, unknown, and illusive as the banks of the Amazon. I could still smell her scent, which sent a shiver of excitement through me. I wanted her again. For a moment, I felt angry that she'd deserted me, left the bed where something bright and wonderful had happened.

Feeling like a college boy after conquering the Homecoming Queen, I strutted into the bathroom, humming *I Believe In Miracles ... Where'd you come from, you sexy thing*. If I was dreaming, I didn't want to wake up. It was all too beautiful and grand. *Let me remain in this reverie until she returns.*

"She'll be back," I said to my reflection in the bathroom mirror. "She has to come back."

I looked into my bathroom mirror. A somewhat drawn and world weary, yet still handsome face looked back. But there was a renewed twinkling in the eye. And along with the gleam came a wild, surging feeling not experienced since my early dating days when I waited on someone's doorstep, or later, when a woman first entered my bedroom.

As I turned on the water for my bath, a crash broke the spell. I walked warily into the living room. On the hearth of the fireplace lay the French ceramic stein. This time it had been hurled against the brickwork, shattering into a hundred pieces.

I immediately called Butch, not to share my escapade, but to get Mama Shari's number.

Mama agreed to see me early that evening. It had to be early so I could be home for Michelle's return. The antics of my house had taken the luster off my new romance and that angered me.

By the afternoon, my elation of the morning had turned into downright depression when Michelle called to tell me she wouldn't be back right away. There were things she needed to get straightened out with her roommate. I'd have to wait another night or two. I wanted so much for our encounter to be real, and for the pleasures of the previous night to be repeated over and over. Boy, was I hooked.

CHAPTER 5

"Forces outside ourselves can greatly influence our thoughts and actions, Mr. Pierson."

Mama Shari wasn't what I'd expected. She was an intelligent, sophisticated woman possessing an exotic moniker. She was closer to the traditional shrink I'd wanted to avoid than she was to a voodoo priestess. Her nickname had come from years in the South, being known as *a seer*. She'd hoped I wasn't disappointed by the lack of charms and incense.

"I am convinced, through a lifetime of experience, that the power of the mind far exceeds what science has been able to prove or grasp. Let me clarify what I believe before I try to make sense of what's happening to you. There are imprints made on the world during our lives, and also images left behind when we are gone. We're not talking about the occult, or spirits from Heaven or Hell. Basically, all energy goes to the same place, and may or may not manifest itself in another being at another time. There's nothing spooky about it. It's just the way things work.

"Now, about your situation. Objects moving and changing shape, seeing things that shouldn't be, and beginning a relationship that would be considered taboo by many. All of this is less unusual than you might think, and there *are* rational explanations. Not ones that science or most people would be happy with, but ones that fit into the rational order of things."

Mama had a confident and soothing bedside manner. I felt I was getting a history lesson rather than psychoanalysis. I liked that.

"First, from what you've described, I believe that your mind, along with some force outside yourself, has caused this kinetic activity. But the sources could be many. It may be that the imprint of your wife's passing was so strong on your subconscious that it created an environment of disharmony."

"Can you give that to me in words I can understand, Mama?"

"A strong residue of your wife's existence, working in conjunction with your subconscious has created the power to change things."

"So maybe my wife's ghost is haunting, rearranging, and breaking things to aggravate the hell out of me?"

"Not exactly. I don't buy into the haunting aspect. It's not so much the power beyond the grave as residual energy."

"But it seems like it comes down to the same thing."

"Remember, however, that it doesn't have to be frightening. You can overcome your fears by accepting the disharmony and, in effect, cut the energy cord that causes these events. To reiterate, I believe what has happened in your case is that a combination of your creative mind, mixed with the strong impression your wife left behind, and perhaps, an unresolved conflict in your past have all come together to produce paranormal phenomena. A realization of these factors will allow you to accept what rationally can't be explained and will, in time, disappear when they no longer have an emotional hold on you."

"Butch said you had a client affected by someone still alive?"

"That was true in Norma's case and that's another possibility, although I don't think it's true in your case. I also believe strongly in the power of suggestion and, to some extent, thought-alteration. As I said when we started, forces beyond ourselves can affect our thoughts."

"Now it sounds like voodoo dolls or mind control."

"That's not far off. Commonly, people believe in things that aren't part of the larger reality. Madison Avenue is a master of this technique. If a thought is placed in your reality, it's just as real as that chair you're sitting in.

"Getting back to Norma's case, through the power of concentration and pressing the right buttons, a rival for her position was able to make Norma believe that her life was a mess and she almost quit her job. This rival could have quite possibly driven her to suicide."

"So, what happened?"

"After offering my bit of observation and advice, she was able to understand how powers exerted by others created this environment in her mind. Now, she's back to her old self and kicking butt. Her supposed friend's attempt failed once Norma had a new understanding of the atmosphere telepathy was capable of creating."

"It all sounds encouraging and maybe I'm not crazy after all, but I still wonder about the photos and Michelle."

"You have the power to actually superimpose her image onto your photos. You, for whatever reason—conflict, loneliness, or empty nest syndrome—created an image you found pleasing. I'd be willing to bet that your Michelle didn't look exactly like the image you created initially, but now, having met this girl, the pictures match perfectly."

I shook my head, confused. "Does the government know about his form of mind control, you think?"

"Sure they do, but I wouldn't trust them to be wise enough to use it successfully." Mama chuckled. "Don't let me get you all shook up, Mr. Pierson. People affect the physical world through the paranormal all the time without even realizing it. It's the natural order of things, if only we knew how to quantify it. I know how frightening it must have been to witness changes and destruction, and without understanding, any normal human would think he was insane. Sanity lies on a continuum we all fall onto, to a greater or lesser degree. Saneness is subjective and consequently overrated. There are more things in the universe unseen than seen, believe me."

Smiling and dumbly nodding this time, I told her I'd try to process all the information and hoped it would help me get over the feeling that someone, or some thing wanted to do me harm.

"Just keep an open mind, always," she said. Standing and taking my hands in hers, she added, "Mr. Pierson, don't feel guilty about your new relationship. You're a lucky man, I'd say. Enjoy, and if, or when it ends, don't go into a funk. That might put your mugs, or toys, or whatever right in bed with you."

Driving home, I felt relieved and made up my mind not to second-guess why Michelle came along. Our relationship possessed its own momentum and I was more than happy to let it carry me along on a current that might lead into deeper waters. You only live once and I had been lucky enough to receive a bonus. *Enjoy* would be my mantra. For each day this beautiful creature graced my life, I would be glad and rejoice.

When it came to personal information, such as numbers and addresses, Michelle had been illusive. Waiting and wondering about her could have torn me apart if I had let it, but even if it all turned out to be a one night stand, then I had to cherish that memory.

I went about my business as normally as possible for two long days. Then, on the third night after her first visit, she again appeared on the doorstep with her two suitcases as promised.

"I talked to my mom and she reluctantly approved of my moving in with you," she said, coming inside.

"Mother knows best," I replied, trying to be cool and keep my hands off of her.

"Everything is straightened out now. So, here I am and I'm all yours, if you still want me."

I wasn't going to ask what she'd straightened out although it was my nature to gather details. Not this time, I decided. I was sticking to my ironclad mantra of *Enjoy, Enjoy*. If she wanted to share her life with me, fine, and I'd settle for what she chose to reveal.

"I've made room in my closet for your things whenever you want to get organized."

"Later, Captain," she said surreptitiously. "Let's organize later. How about we rearrange each other for now."

We didn't make it to the bedroom. We made love on the floor of the living room. I now wondered what I would do without her. Playing on my vulnerability, she had already become a surrogate wife, and answered some of the questions Mama Shari had raised about being alone. No longer was that Raymond Chandler scene of a lonely guy appealing. My craving for now lay beneath me.

After rising to the occasion more often than I thought possible, we went to bed. I slept like a dead man, with no worrisome dreams or fears about what my house's reaction would be.

The next morning, as Michelle lay sleeping, I got up, found my robe, and headed first for the john, then the living room. Almost tripping over her luggage, setting where she'd left it, I opened the door to get the newspaper. A man stood across the street. He was middle-aged, of medium height, and beginning to lose his hair. There was nothing unusual about him other than there being no discernable reason for his presence. We made eye contact for a moment and then he turned and sauntered down the sidewalk.

Rescuing the paper from my driveway, I made some coffee, put Stan Getz in the CD player, and listened to his mellow sax play *Fly Me To The Moon*. I waited, almost expecting something paranormal to happen. But maybe my session with Mama *had* put my mind on a path of greater understanding that would chase away whatever imagery existed.

I scanned the paper, listened to the music, and contemplated life until Michelle emerged from the bedroom wearing just her panties. Looking at her and still wanting to pinch myself, I wondered if this could really be my new life standing before me.

She came over to the back of my chair and put her arms around my neck. "How's stuff?" she asked.

"I think I might have seen your stalker," I told her.

CHAPTER 6

To my surprise, there were no surprises for two solid, wonderful weeks. With the exception of Michelle's occasional disappearing acts, causing me to speculate on what she was up to while gone, life and lovemaking were scintillating. She'd questioned me about the man I saw outside the house and dismissed it when my description didn't match her visitor. She said he hadn't returned to her shop since she had moved in with me.

Everything played copasetic, so much so that I didn't care to leave the house. I wanted to be there whenever she arrived. I'd suggested meeting for lunch, but she said I'd get tired of her if we overdid it. I also wanted to do some photos, but she hadn't made the time.

She had been as mystified as I by her appearance in the foothills photos. "I must have an unknown twin sister," she had comically commented.

Never coming right out and asking how she spent her time—except for school or work—I wondered if she had another guy, some young beefcake with which she was balancing the scales. But really, it was none of my business, and I knew if I wanted to keep her it had to be with an open hand. If she suddenly flew away like a bird, so be it. But when we were together, our lovemaking seemed to me like nuclear fission, hitting previously unreachable high notes, and our conversations were intelligent and meaningful.

While basking in the radiance of this woman's affections, I'd almost forgotten about my son's graduation. I wanted Michelle to be part of all the things I cherished. I invited her to the ceremony. She said she would check her schedule.

Nothing lasts forever I suppose, and eventually my house seemed to wake up from a temporary slumber. It was as if it said to me, "So you think you're Joe Cool and just perfectly normal, eh?" That same day, something told me to check Ryan's former room, which contained mostly sports memorabilia from his high school days. I went through his room with caution. I studied his trophies and team pictures, and at first glance, saw nothing amiss. On the way out, his last high school portrait caught my eye. Across my son's face was scrawled the words, "Stop Her," in black marker. Michelle had not been in the room, I felt sure, and so it wasn't a simple prank.

The other shoe had finally dropped, I reckoned, but rather than experience fear, I felt rage well up inside. I was in no mood for rain to fall on my parade. "What do you want? What are you trying to tell me?" I shouted, still looking at the writing. "Spell it out?"

I looked around the room again for further signs or messages. I found none. Would I ever find an answer? I wanted to tell Michelle about this. Maybe she could even shed some light. Nothing had ever happened while she was in residence. Maybe she would eventually be around more often.

***

I decided not discuss the incident with Michelle, not yet. Instead, I followed her one morning. Doubt still lingered about her presence in my life. Could she be causing these things? I hoped against hope the answer would be, "No."

Not knowing where she worked, I waited in the school parking lot. After several hours, she emerged with another girl. They were laughing and talking like a couple of college girls as they crossed the black asphalt to their respective cars. I knew then I wasn't cut out for surveillance work. My *keister* felt like it had been dipped in concrete from being in one spot for so long.

The girls separated. As I watched Michelle get into her hatchback, I knew there was something different about her. Somehow she wasn't as pretty. Maybe I'd forgotten to wear my rose colored glasses. She pulled out, headed for downtown. It was going to be tricky, following her in Denver traffic.

Losing her once, I luckily spotted her compact turn into an all-day lot in the heart of the city. Now came the tough part—finding my own spot without losing sight of her. I'd concocted a cover story in case she noticed me and pulled into a loading zone until I saw her enter a floral shop on the Sixteenth Street Mall. I put the Jag in a lot and found myself a burger stand where I could watch the shop's entrance.

I watched, and watched, and waited. She never came out. After a while, I strolled past the place and peered inside. Finally, my curiosity getting the better of me, I said, "To hell with it" and went in. Seeing no one, I walked to the back of the room till I reached a drawn curtain. Opening it slightly to peek in, a severe, unpleasant face stared back at me, eyeball to eyeball.

"May I help you?" said a wrinkled older lady.

Dropping my cover story like a hot rock, I asked, "Is Michelle in?"

"Michelle left hours ago. Can I help you with something?" she said sternly.

Shit. "No thanks," I said, and made a beeline to the door, feeling the woman's eyes burning a hole in the back of my head.

How could she have given me the slip? I checked the lot and sure enough, her car was gone. Driving home, I'd been glad for the second time I hadn't tried to make my living at undercover work.

Michelle's car sat in my driveway. This would be a first, *my* coming home to *her*. At first, I thought my belongings had done some marching around the living room. Then I realized Michelle had made some changes.

She had done something special. She had purchased candles, which I didn't keep around, had placed them attractively around the room, and decanted a nice bottle of wine. Curled up on my couch, she was waiting for me, as fetching as ever.

"So, what have you been up to, big boy?" she asked.

"Hey, don't I get to have some secrets too?"

"Come here. I want to show you something,"

Obeying, I sat down next to her. "Are we having a special occasion with the candlelight and wine?"

"Every night is special with you. But I do have something new. I hope you approve."

She stood in front of me and wriggled her jeans and panties down to her thighs. A small tattoo graced her lower torso, just above her pubic hairline and to the left of center. It was two tiny stars tied in a bow.

"Two bright stars tied together in my flesh forever. *Tied* together. Get it?"

I got it. I'd never been a fan of permanent markings on one's body, but how could I not be impressed with the representation of my name, especially there, where everyone she had sex with the rest of her life would see it and ask about it. I covered the green stars with my lips.

"Can you handle my kind of love and affection, Ty?"

I looked up at her and saw the impish siren I would gladly dash my ship against the rocks for. "I can handle it," I said breathily and buried my face in the pink petals beneath her dark triangle of love.

There were no more questions that evening. And finally, Michelle fell asleep wearing only the new gift she had bought her body.

CHAPTER 7

I had not seen Ryan for over two months. He'd been busy with finals and the car incident had landed him a new girl friend. Michelle had been with me for three weeks and I still hadn't the occasion to mention her to my son.

When we finally talked, he must have read my mind. "What's the matter, Pops? Got a girlfriend and afraid to tell me?"

"Sort of," I answered, "but she's nothing like what you'd expect."

"Bring her up for graduation with you. We all can celebrate."

"I plan on taking you out whether Michelle comes along or not. What about this girlfriend of yours? I thought you were seeing someone named Holly."

"Old news, Dad. When Mallory ran into me, it was the best thing that ever happened. She is so awesome."

I'll match my girl with your girl any time, my boy, I thought, smugly. "Well great," I said. What class is she in?"

"She's graduating too. That's why I want us to celebrate."

"Are her folks going to be there?"

"No. They're out-of-state and can't make it."

"Okay, okay. I'll take you guys out for a nice dinner. You pick the place."

"All right. All I can say is, wait till you get a load of her."

"So tell me what's so special?"

"She's beautiful, about five and a half feet, dark hair and eyes, and *soooo* hot."

"She sounds sizzling. Remember to be careful though."

"Christ Dad, I'm not stupid."

"Well, I'll look forward to meeting her."

"She even says she's going to figure out some way to have me be a part of her, permanently, like a tattoo or something."

I stared at a wall. Ryan was still talking, but I wasn't processing what he was saying. My senses had shut down.

"Dad, did you hear me?"

"What's her name again?" I finally said.

"Mallory ... Smith. Why?"

"Are you with her most of the time?"

"Yeah ... Not all the time. We get together a couple of times a week. She works and is too busy for much dating. What's up with you?"

"Nothing." Trying to end the conversation normally, I said, "Well, congratulations, college grad. I'll plan on seeing you next Saturday."

"Okay, Pops. Later."

No way in hell, I told myself. *No way.* It's a coincidence. Got to be. Besides, Michelle is twenty-five. This girl is probably Ryan's age.

The phone rang again, making me jump.

"Hello?"

Only a steady, buzzing, electronic sound.

"Yes?"

Nothing more. The low buzzing continued. Caller ID said "UNKNOWN." The sound gave me chills. I thought I could hear a faint voice, but it sounded robotic—God, I tried not to think this—like something from the grave. I listened intently. Through the electronic interference, I thought I heard "*staaaap herrrrrr.*" I took the phone from my ear and gently put it down like nothing had happened, trying to ignore the fact that I was trembling.

The phone rang again, sending a second shot of electricity through me. "BLOCKED," Caller ID said. *Just someone selling something this time. Something ordinary.*

On the fourth ring, I grabbed the dastardly instrument.

"Thrill me " I uttered, almost shouting.

"Can't help you there Ty-man. You soliciting now?"

"Butch, damn it, the phone's been giving me fits," I said, relieved to hear his voice. "How's it hanging?"

"Long, hairy, and hard to carry."

I laughed nervously.

"Say, are you bagging your old buddy? I thought by now I'd hear about your visit with Mama and what happened with your rock-chick. What's up with you?"

"Yeah, sorry I haven't called. Thought you might have heard about my seeing Mama," I said, lamely.

"I don't hear shit, man, unless the ex calls to unload on me. So, did she paint your ass, or what?"

"No, she had some good advice, I guess. How about coming over one night this week. We'll drink and catch up."

"Lots to tell, huh? Let's do Wednesday. Want to grab a bite first?"

"No, I'll feed you. Besides, I have someone I want you to meet."

"Something tells me you're finally gettin' some tail. That might explain why I haven't heard from you."

"I'll tell you about it Wednesday," I said, trying to put some humor in my voice. "About eight?"

"Cool. I'll be on pins and needles."

Talking to Butch always grounded me. I liked the understanding we had. If one of us had someone over, we took care of him, none of this what-can-I-bring bullshit. You took care of each other. Thinking about discussing the last few weeks with Butch helped me dismiss the first call with Ryan, and took my mind off the second call with the electronic voice from beyond, beyond.

Fixing a bite, I wondered if Michelle would be coming home. I fought with the idea that she could be in Boulder. "Stop it, fool," I said, like Butch would say it, and poured myself a nasty one.

Michelle did come in that night, quite late. Waking me when she climbed into bed, she told me she couldn't go to Boulder the following Saturday, but seemed delighted for the opportunity to meet one of my friends. She was probably thought I didn't have any. At least she could see she wasn't the only person in my life.

I also told her about the weird call and how eerie it was.

"Maybe it's your wife calling from the beyond to tell you to get rid of the young chick you're screwing."

"That's not funny, Michelle. Not funny at all." I turned away, mad that she had been so flippant about the incident. The comment had also scared me, since I'd had the same thought.

"Hey, lover," she said, touching my cheek. "I didn't mean to be disrespectful. Really." Then she nestled against me, willing to endure my mood.

Not wanting to be silly about it, I took her in my arms. "It's okay. It's just that a lot of mysterious things have been happening lately and frankly, you're the biggest mystery of all. You can't blame me for wondering where you are and what you do? I'm not asking that you tell me, I just worry about you."

"Don't," she declared. "I'm here now and you've got me, and I want to make it up to you for what I said."

She reached under the covers and all my fears melted away.

✳✳✳

The last thing I remember before falling asleep was that my chest lay against Michelle's back. My heart thumped to the same rhythm as hers, making me feel all the more that somehow the two of us belonged together. I awoke in the predawn hours to find Michelle's side of the bed empty and it frightened me. I was fearful that she had left again, yet the space where she had lain was still warm.

I climbed out of bed to search for her and found her in my study looking at the trinkets on my desk. She stood naked. I momentarily wondered if she might be sleepwalking. Observing her in the dim light, her body seemed flawless. Her shoulder, back, buttocks, and legs belonged in an artist's sketchbook. I again wondered how I had been fortunate enough to captivate one so perfect, a woman out of a dream, while at the same time harboring the feeling that there was something she was hiding, some great mystery I was not at all sure I cared to unravel.

She finally turned. In all the beauty of her nakedness, she seemed to be examining me. A slight, conspiratorial smile crept across he face. "Lover," she said as sweetly as a classical note on a violin.

"Is everything all right?" I asked.

She was holding the totem pole from my desk in her delicate hands. "Off course. Everything is progressing nicely."

"Are you eventually coming back to bed?"

Never had I seen movement as sensual as the sight of Michelle gliding silently across the floor toward me. She seemed to study the lines on my face. I started to feel uncomfortable under her scrutiny, but then she wrapped her arms around my neck.

"Say you want to be with me," she said, her warm breath on my shoulder. Her delicate cheek rested against my chest. I felt her nipples begin to stiffen as they lightly brushed against me.

"I want you more than I've ever wanted anything, Michelle. I would like it if you never left my sight."

In spite of the fact that I was becoming aroused again, it was as if I was consoling a child, offering her security. Once more I wondered about motive, then banished such thoughts. "Come back to bed with me," I said to her.

"I'll do anything you want. I will please you exactly as you instruct, but you must love me forever."

"Tell me you're not a ghost." The words were surprisingly out of my mouth before I could bite them off.

That quizzical expression crossed her face again. "Where do you get such notions?" She brought her lips up to mine and kissed me deeply, passionately. "Does that feel like the lips of a ghost?" She rubbed the totem and her hand against my genitals. "Or this?"

I did instruct her and found her more aggressive than any woman I had ever been with. Our coupling was more intense than ever before. It was as if she suddenly needed to experience everything before time ran out on us. I also felt that our spirits had somehow locked together along with our bodies, and felt no matter what happened, I would never be without Michelle completely.

***

A late spring shower hit the city the following day. Michelle didn't want to get out of bed. Usually she was up and gone early. It would have been the perfect sort of day to stay in bed with her, but I had ants in my pants and the buzzing phone from the night before still had me on edge.

Deciding to show Michelle that I not only had other people in my life, but also other things to concern myself with, I decided to knock out some errands. If I got out for a while, maybe it would chase the blues. Then, I could spend the afternoon in bed, looking for new ways to explore her.

Even as the Jag's engine hummed to life, I thought of going back inside ... to spend every possible moment with her. Before Michelle, I'd achieved some level of sad contentment, but her presence had changed my equation for living. There was more than mere contentment. Pleasure and pain traveled through my spirit like dazzling colored lights through a prism. I found myself in the front car of a roller-coaster, at the zenith one moment when holding Michelle, our limbs entwined blissfully as she whispered sweet nothings in my ear, then plummeting down ... down into my journey's nadir on the nights she did not come home.

I sometimes wondered if this wild ride of emotions would careen off the tracks of my heretofore-structured life into a world where voices whispered in my ear and on the telephone, only to be silenced by the undulations and moans of my beautiful nymph.

When it ended, as surely it would, could I amble on, shooting my meaningless pictures, paying bills, returning to the mundane world of mere contentment? I knew I couldn't. I'd reached a new realm of existence, more profound with the highs and the lows. I didn't believe I could go on without her.

With a will, I backed out of the drive, leaving Michelle to dream and prayed she would be there when I returned. My first stop was the neighborhood grocery. As I walked across the lot toward the entrance, someone grabbed my arm. I turned to face the man who had been standing in front of my house weeks before.

"We need to talk," he said, holding onto my arm as if he was afraid I'd get away.

"Who are you?" I asked, pulling my arm free.

"I'm Michelle's father. Let's grab a cup of coffee. Please, do that much for me."

A Dunkin Donuts nearby provided shelter from the steady downpour. I couldn't tell if this man wanted to scold me, threaten me, or give me a sound thrashing. We got two coffees and took a booth in the back of the shop.

"How long have you been hanging around my house?" I asked, nervously shifting my weight.

"If you're going to turn this into something I've done wrong, Mr. Pierson, forget it."

I didn't want to play who-had-done-what-to-whom. "Why do we need to do this? Have you talked to your daughter?"

"Of course I've talked to her. And what I want to know is what kind of spell have you cast on her?"

"Me? A spell?" I repeated, mystified. If anything, I would have thought it was the other way around. "Mr. Devin, is it?"

He nodded.

"I'm sorry, but I don't have a clue as to what you mean. If you're referring to our attraction ..."

"That's not it," he interrupted. "I've followed her to your house and I've seen her leave the next morning. The person that comes out isn't the same person that goes in."

I just looked at him, wondering if all the light bulbs in his chandelier were screwed in. "I don't follow you."

He sipped his coffee and glanced out at the rain. I had a feeling I was about to learn more about Michelle than I'd ever dreamed. He made an exasperated gesture with his hands and began to speak.

"Michelle has always been a sweet girl, a good student, always conscientious. She's also on the shy side. Frankly, not the kind of girl that would take up with a man older than her own father."

I was thinking that he didn't know his daughter nearly as well as he thought.

"Getting this master's degree is very important to her," he continued, "but suddenly, she's with you and her grades have gone to hell and she's missing time at work."

I sipped my drink and let him vent, hoping my chance to defend Michelle would come.

"What I want to know is, what happens to her when she spends time with you? Michelle is attractive, in her own way, but to be honest, a little frumpy. But when she leaves your place, she comes out looking like a million dollars. Sophisticated. Like she's had a makeover. I know you're not some kind of Svengali who makes a habit of doing young girls. I've checked you out."

Now my pride was being attacked. *Don't push me too hard.*

Mr. Devin took a sip of coffee and continued. "Michelle's not the kind of girl to take up with an older man at the expense of her dreams and ambitions. I know her well enough to know that."

"You already said that. I can understand your feelings. I don't have a daughter, but I have a young son so I can somewhat put myself in your place. You say you've talked to her. Obviously, this is not a problem for Michelle. What does she tell you?"

"That's just it. She doesn't tell me anything about you because she denies knowing you. She has blackouts for periods of time, she's told me, and has no recollection of your relationship. During the times I know she's with you, she claims to be at her apartment. Total denial."

"Wait a minute," I said. "Michelle doesn't have an apartment any more. She had that guy stalking her, so she moved her stuff in with me. Someone's a little confused."

"And that someone is you. You don't know her as well as you think. No one is stalking her and she has the same apartment and roommate she's had for a year. I dropped by just a few days ago and asked about her luggage. She had no idea what had happened to it. She figured she'd left it with me."

"Now wait," I said again. "You say she denies knowing me or living with me, but she told me she'd discussed it with her mother, and she approved."

"Mr. Pierson, Michelle doesn't have a mother. I've raised her since she was five years old."

I don't know if my mouth literally dropped open, but Mr. Devin looked at me like he'd won some sort of victory. His expression said, "gotcha. You're shacked up with a very disturbed young woman."

Finally I found words. "I can't explain the difference you see in her, or why she's told me these things, but I know she has made me very happy."

"You're saying you've had some kind of epiphany over Michelle?" he smirked.

"I don't understand why our relationship happened and I don't think, for a moment, it'll last forever. I do care for her deeply and I respect her, even if she does have some problems."

"Hell yes, you respect her twenty-five year old body, doing whatever the two of you do."

"That's uncalled for, Devin. I've tried to be pleasant about this. I told you we care for each other and I'm going to talk to her about some of these things. But remember, she's an adult and has the right to hang around with my old set of bones if she chooses. But since you're her father, I'll give you the courtesy of asking you what exactly you would have me do?"

"I'd have you change the locks and bolt the door so I can have my daughter back. Not this person who blacks out and then is somehow transformed."

"I can't let her go right now. We're not breaking any laws."

"Well, you've listened," he said with what I'd call dread and dismay in his voice. "I guess that's all I can expect from you. But something isn't right and if you honestly don't know what, I recommend you do some soul searching because its not my daughter who's inside your house."

Mr. Devin stood up and pulled a photo from his inside breast pocket. He handed me the picture of a girl. She smiled at the camera from the piece of paper. She had dark hair and pretty eyes, but it wasn't a picture of my Michelle.

"That's the daughter I know. God knows what kind of demon inside her is changing her when she's with you."

In Devin's attempt to come between Michelle and me, he'd provided me with a moral basis for my desire—to set her free from a delusional father. He took the picture from my hand and walked out into the rain, leaving me with my thoughts and a cold cuppa joe.

CHAPTER 8

Was the whole world crazy or just me? Inquiring mind or not, I didn't relish having to deal with the many contradictions presented, so I put off talking to Michelle about meeting her dad.

The evening Butch planned to come over; I again struggled with contradictions Devin had thrown at me. How could I buy into this business of someone inhabiting someone else? I was an educated and somewhat sophisticated man. Ghosts exist no farther than one's mind allows them to. Some of what Mama had said made unconventional sense, but it depended heavily on the supernatural. Being rational brought little comfort. There are times you have to believe what can't be understood, what isn't rational, no matter how cynical you may be.

More and more, in a scenario that three months earlier I would have believed impossible, my refuge became Michelle's warmth. In her arms I was transformed, redeemed of my shortcomings. I could block out the rest of existence. Having Michelle act as if we were the only two people in the world was the rock around which my reality now revolved, the only time I didn't fear for my sanity.

Facing everything else became increasingly problematic. Even though it would be good to see Butch, I was sorry I had invited him, wondering what the effect his presence would have on my bumps in the night.

"Trick or treat?" He was carrying a bottle of *Courvoisier*. "A house warming gift for you and the little lady."

"Hey, thanks. You always buy the best. We'll get into it tonight, Hoss."

"So where is fair lady?"

"Michelle isn't home yet, but promised she'd make it before you left. She's young and independent. What can I tell you?"

"Hey man, I'm new to Peyton Place. Give me a chance to pick up on the plot here. Bring me up-to-date."

We set the cognac aside for later and had a couple of beers. I regurgitated the highlights of Mama Shari's analysis, and of Michelle's mysterious, convoluted history, including the altercation with her father.

"Don't mention this stuff when she gets here," I cautioned. "I'm still trying to figure out how to approach the subject."

Butch gave me a sly, nonplussed gaze. "Man, sounds like you've got one dizzy dame on your hands. Is she really worth it?"

"Wait till you meet her. You can decide."

We had steaks for dinner, talked and relaxed. It felt good. Life felt normal. With a beer and two Jack Daniels put away, I told him about the stein shattering, the writing on Ryan's picture, and the voice on the phone.

"Sounds like things have really gotten fucked up since this romance started."

"Maybe so, but it's Michelle who provides the stability now," I said, looking him straight in the eye.

"*Ooooweeee*, Tyster. This is one for Stephen King. I think you better sell this story to somebody."

"That's an idea. Maybe I—"

A loud crash made me jump and slosh my drink. It came from the master bedroom. I looked at Butch and he stared back at me as if all his teasing was coming back to haunt him.

I rose and calmly walked to the bedroom door. One of Michelle's suitcases, which had sat empty on the closet floor, now lay on top of the mirrored vanity. The suitcase had apparently hurdled across the room and shattered the mirror upon impact.

"Come look at this," I said to Butch.

Reluctantly obeying, he stared silently at this mischief. "I will never, ever watch *Poltergeist* again, brother. This is some serious shit. I think you ought to pack the fuck up and move in with me. Or … maybe not with me, but move somewhere "

I contemplated this latest assault wondering if I was being too wimpy, allowing myself to be at this phenomena's mercy. I thought about shouting, "Be gone from this house, devil spirits," or something equally inane.

"You're smiling," Butch said incredulously. "What'cha smiling at, man? This is one crazy mother-fucking deal here "

"You've seen it."

"Yeah?"

"So if I'm nuts, so are you. I've got a witness now."

"Yeah, I've seen it and I don't like it, so let's both get our crazy asses out of here and call Ghostbusters."

"Calm down, buddy. It's just natural phenomena. All we have to do is learn how to interpret it."

"Natural my black ass! Ain't nothin' natural about this shit."

"Hey!"

Butch and I jumped a couple of inches as Michelle stood behind us. She had sneaked in quietly while we were occupied with the bedroom mirror.

"Jesus Christ, Michelle You scared the crap out of us."

She smiled, pleased with herself. "What are you fellows doing peeking into the bedroom anyway?"

"Lady, do you always get fireworks before your arrival?"

"You must be Butch?" She shoved a slender hand out to him. "What happened?"

"Oh, just your usual flying objects breaking things, flying glass, stuff that happens when you're not around," I answered.

She looked in the bedroom, then back at me.

"Damn," she said. "No more watching in the mirror for awhile, babe," she added, shrugging. "What are you going to do?"

"Keep you around more often," I said.

"I hope this won't frighten you off?" Michelle said to Butch. "Ty needs his friends."

Butch raised his hands in mock terror. "Hey, I'd love to hang with you and Ty ... but ... you've got to get yourself despooked."

Michelle and I laughed. What else could we do?

Butch hung around, but when he wasn't studying Michelle, his eyes darted around the room. Jokingly, he had asked me if Ryan had a football helmet he could wear. In spite of the incident, we were able to lighten up and enjoy each other's company, drink the *Courvoisier* and get snockered. Michelle squeezed next to me and we delighted in some of Butch's crazy stories about when he and I had worked together. Walking him to the door around midnight, I asked what he thought of Michelle.

He lowered his eyes and stared at the floor for a moment, then looked at me again and said, "She's a looker, my man. No doubt. And she dig's your ass, obviously. She crawls all over you like a spider after the fly in a web."

"Yeah, so what do you think?"

"I'll be straight with you. I'd be the same way if I were in your shoes, but I think you should watch your back. You're a cool dude and I'm glad you're having fun with her, but don't make her your world. And you've got to find out what's up with this paranormal business."

"Okay," I said. "Suggestions duly noted."

"I want you around. Be careful."

"We'll talk," I said.

Off he strolled into the night.

Michelle had disappeared into the shower and I could swear I heard her talking to someone. I went to the bathroom door to listen. Sensing my presence, she slid the shower door open.

"Want to join me?" she asked, standing there in all her glory. "I'll scrub your back."

"Sure," I said, "but who were you talking to?"

"Uh oh. You're eavesdropping on my private conversations. I talk to the walls when I'm trying to figure things out, like your poltergeist."

Undressing in the bedroom, I again viewed the damage that had to be cleaned up, but the steam of the shower was the stronger lure for my tired mind and body. As I climbed in, I asked Michelle if she was upset by the incident in the bedroom.

"Yes, I am. Especially because we won't be able to watch ourselves making love," she said, trying to brighten my spirits. "Maybe it should be replaced with an overhead mirror."

"Oh yeah, and have that come crashing down."

"These strange happenings will go away. I don't know why I'm so sure, I just am. So, don't let it get you down. Let me take care of you," she whispered, covering me in soapsuds. "You're friend's a riot. I like him. I hope he liked me. Did he?"

"He said you were spectacular," I answered, while wondering if my house would be haunted forever.

✳✳✳

One night I awoke, thinking Michelle lay next to me. I felt the touch of fingers against my face and in my hair. I reached over to return the gentle touches, but no one was there. The only thing with which I shared my bedroom was the deadly quiet.

Alone again in my house. My spirits sagged somewhat at the new emptiness. Something nameless and faceless had touched me. I hated the thought that my mind could play such tricks. Lying there, I scanned my surroundings. Everything in its place, no moving objects to accompany the gentle touches. They'd been like a caress, a slow, lingering lovers touch.

I momentarily wondered if the time would come when I'd be too terrified to come home alone without Michelle waiting to receive me. Up until now, it surprised me that I wasn't more frightened. Fright speeds up the heart and gets the adrenalin pumping, but I was strangely calm. Changes were taking place, no doubt, but I didn't suffer from a weak heart and I wasn't a frail person to be terrorized by something unknown. I could be as cavalier as Michelle, I'd decided. In spite of broken mirrors and steins, nothing had happened to cause me physical injury.

Keeping that in mind, I got up and walked into my makeshift darkroom. I studied the photos of Michelle among the boulders from every angle. She was solidly there with that strange smile. Still, there was something elusive, even in the photos. She had the aura of a fine mist that could enter your pores and find your soul. The feeling was that of an emersion into an all-encompassing relationship, but with one party not totally there. It gave me the shivers and led my mind to wonder just how Michelle and the moving objects were connected.

There is some kind of geometry to the universe for everything that happens, understood or not, I told myself. Even Mama Shari would agree, and although Michelle's photos, Michelle herself, and the activities of wandering spirits did not provide much confidence of ever again being rational, I accepted the immersion that would never allow me to see the world in the same way again.

I left the pictures, the darkroom, and went about my day doing what I always did, and tried to ignore the sensation of being observed.

CHAPTER 9

I drove to Boulder alone.

The campus crawled with a myriad of activity, with friends and relatives of students everywhere. I briefly met with Ryan before the ceremony. His girl, Mallory, was busy elsewhere, but I'd see her when she received her sheepskin. I told Ryan how proud of him I was and asked where we'd be going for dinner. Then he was off. I found a seat offering a reasonable view between the hats of two ladies in the row in front of me.

Carol and I were college grads. We hadn't known each other in school because she was three years younger and went to college in a different state. But college had been fun for both of us and this would have been a momentous occasion if she were alive.

Sitting there about to see our son graduate, I felt melancholy. I wished terribly that she were here to see him. I also felt ashamed because I'd hardly given her a thought since meeting Michelle. I wiped a tear away at that realization.

The PA system came on, too loud like always, and the program began. Sitting there listening to the speakers, looking at the tops of one thousand mortarboards, I thought I heard someone whispering in my ear. The sound was similar to the one on the phone: a sizzling electronic sound, floating on the wind and into my head. "*Saaaave himmmm,*" it was saying. "*Saaaave himmmm.*"

I looked around at the other parents. People were applauding as diplomas were handed out. To everyone else, all was normal. I put my pinky in my ear like I was mining for earwax, hoping for better reception, or that the sound would go away.

It abruptly stopped, but a foreboding suddenly gripped and held on to me. I was convinced that when Mallory Smith walked across the stage to accept her diploma, it would be Michelle Devin I'd see.

The names rolled by. Collins ... Jacobsen ... Neville ... Then, Pierson ... Ryan Pierson. Ryan crossed the platform. He smiled and held up a fist in victory. *We did it, Carol.* And then the name, Saunders. I began to sweat even though it was a cool day. Then, Greg Smith. Then, Mallory Smith. I didn't want to look, but I forced myself. I saw an attractive profile, a cute face, with dark hair falling from beneath her cap onto the shoulder of her gown. She was beautiful in her own way, but it was *not* Michelle.

Exhaling a sigh and wondering what had gotten into me, I applauded the remaining graduates. Still, there had been the voice. Not to worry, I decided. I was going to have a great time with my kid and his girl.

✱✱✱

We drove to a steak house Ryan had chosen. Mallory was charming and mature beyond her years. She retold the fender-bender story saying that if she'd known my son, she would have run into him long ago. Ryan had lined up a good entry-level job as a copy boy and part-time feature writer for a Boulder paper. Mallory was looking for a high school teaching position. They were a good-looking couple and I wished I could have shown off Michelle. The four of us, I thought, would have had a blast. That's what I thought until Mallory got the giggles about something Ryan had said and broke into a high-pitched laugh. More like a cackle.

Goose bumps covered my arms and the hair stood up on my neck. I didn't say anything and laughed along with them, but it was then I realized, once and for all, that somehow by some sorcerer's magic, Michelle Devin was there with my son and I.

My son was being victimized by some kind of charade. He and I were involved somehow with the same being. But how could that be? When Mallory went to powder her nose I had my chance. "Son, did Mallory get a tattoo?"

"Uuhh ... yeah, she did. How'd you know?"

"You told me she was going to do something for you."

I could tell he was embarrassed about telling me the details.

"It's kind of personal, between me and her," he said.

I was pretty certain I knew what the tattoo looked like. Mallory returned and I let it drop.

What I had to accept I knew was impossible, but there it was. In spite of indications to the contrary, I thought of Michelle as an innocent, a woman yet to be completely molded by life. Was it an angel or a devil that had come into my life?

Like Butch had advised, this had to be settled with Michelle. *Stop her* and *Save him* in my head, two similar women, both young and beautiful, the laughs, the tattoos? Michelle's father. Butch's feelings. It was all too much, too unbelievable. No more beating around the bush. When I got home I planned to confront Michelle about everything.

※※※

The house was empty, not to my surprise. How long did it take a spirit or demon to hop from one body to another? I didn't see how Michelle and I could go on unless somebody could explain what was behind these manifestations. Maybe she was protecting us, but from what? I had to find out at the risk of losing her.

That night I pulled out the photos I'd taken of Michelle that first day ... the first day of my new life, and studied them for a third time. I had somehow managed to side step what was clear then, but what my reality refused to accept. I was in love with and making love to a phantom. Yet, I had made love to her, felt my body inside her.

Insanity had been ruled out. The only other rational explanation was that I was lost in a dream without end ... or dead, perhaps. That would give some form and shape to my new reality. When you're dead, there's a new set of rules.

I put down Michelle's pictures and slowly returned from the mysterious abyss of confusion. I checked my Caller ID. Mama Shari had left a message for me to call right away. It was late, but I called anyway.

"Mama? This is Ty Pierson."

"Mr. Pierson, so good to hear from you. I have some information. I don't know if it will mean anything to you but ..."

"Go on," I said.

"Well, it's a little out of my line, but I remembered the advice I gave you about keeping an open mind and I thought I should take my own advice."

I waited.

"Butch called and told me what happened at your home and about the things that have happened since we met. Your case is requiring me to rethink what I've advised you. I've decided that one or more entities from the other side is trying to make contact in rather obvious ways."

"You're telling me," I said, "and it may just be this girl I've taken up with, the one in the pictures. I believe she's the center of what's going on, just like I've allowed her to become the center of my life."

"That may be. I feel I've done you harm by not taking the malevolent factor into account and not providing you with a means to fight it."

"What do you recommend?"

"You must find out why this girl came into your life. That will guide you. The other thing is, I keep seeing something that won't go away. You've been on my mind since talking to Butch. He's very concerned about you. Anyway, I keep seeing a name. Martha Bouchette—Portland.

"I don't understand?"

"When I think of you, Mr. Pierson, I see the name, Martha Bouchette, Portland ... Oregon or Maine, I don't know which. Does the name mean anything to you?"

"Martha ... Martha," I said, searching my memory. "Yes, it does. It's the name of someone I dated years ago, before I met my wife. You just saw this name? How exactly?"

"It's like a newspaper headline, as clear as day."

"How strange ... but what isn't right now. I'll have to think about what it could mean."

"Be careful, Mr. Pierson. Someone or something has a purpose for you, and now I can't be at all sure it's positive."

"I will, Mama. I plan to have a discussion with Michelle about all of this."

"May I offer one last bit of advice?"

"Sure."

"Perhaps you shouldn't show all your cards too quickly. Playing along while you gather information might be prudent, but if you sense physical danger, then, by all means, get away from her."

"Please call again if you ..."

"Have any more visions? This is a new experience for me, so I'm learning as I go. I'll keep in touch, and please proceed carefully."

CHAPTER 10

Michelle had been gone for two days following my trip to Boulder. If I were a betting man, I'd guess she knew I'd figured something out and was lying low. In her absence, I investigated the name Mama had given me. Sometimes the illusion of progress can provide hope, even if it proves to be false hope.

On a library computer, I went back to the mid-seventies and spent two days researching before coming up with anything. Finally, I ran across a twenty-six year old obituary in a Portland, Oregon newspaper on one Martha Elizabeth Bouchette.

Searching the paper prior to that date revealed a brief article on a local woman's suicide and the suffocation death of her daughter. The coroner's ruling was a murder/suicide. The article had little information other than the fact that, *a mother and brother survive Ms. Bouchette.*

In addition, I searched my memory trying to recall everything I could remember about the Martha Bouchette I had known. I had met her not long before meeting Carol. We had dated exclusively for a few months. As I recalled, it had been pretty hot and heavy. But when Carol came along, my attention shifted and Martha and I went our separate ways. I remembered that she had made several attempts to reconcile but Carol had won the battle for my affections.

Even though I hadn't thought of this woman in ages, I felt a twinge of—shall I call it regret—to discover that she too was gone and had been for many years. It made me feel old to know that the last woman with whom I'd been involved prior to my wife was also deceased.

Then, I thought of Michelle. Even though our relationship was in jeopardy, the longer I was away from her, the more I thought I could forgive her anything rather than lose her. Desire and longing, I had found, can make a person blind to facts.

If I sound like someone undeserving of respect and devoid of a backbone when it came to dealing with Michelle, you have to remember how enchanted I was by this vital life force that had dropped in from the blue. She had given me a chance to relive my youth. It was extremely difficult to deal with issues that might cause her to leave.

Suddenly, I had a bright idea. Remembering that Martha had family in Denver, I scanned the phone book. With just a handful of Bouchettes, it didn't take long to score a hit. A cousin, who didn't want to be bothered with family history, told me that Martha's mother was still alive and resided in an area nursing home.

Now my investigation had some legs. I went to bed that evening wondering if Michelle would come in late and wake me like she had so many times, asking if I had missed her. As it turned out, I slept alone, but soundly. My last thought was to wonder what in the world I would ask Mrs. Bouchette about her dead daughter.

***

As I drove to the nursing home, I did the math. Twenty-seven years now since I met Carol, so I was twenty-eight and Martha was about twenty-four, so her mother was probably at least forty-five then. That would put her in her mid-seventies now, or there-abouts.

I parked and went in. A friendly receptionist directed me to the wing where I would find Mrs. Bouchette. A not-so-friendly nurse aide led me to room 313. As we walked towards the room, the familiar nursing home smell rolled over me in waves, the unpleasant odors of unwashed hair and stale urine. Ryan once called it the smell of old ass. My mother too had spent her last years in a place similar to Shady Grove.

Mrs. Bouchette occupied one-half of a small lavender, cinderblock room she shared with another resident. Either my calculations were off at least a decade or a difficult life had aged her beyond her years. She sat in a rocker next to her bed.

I pulled the only other chair on her side of the room close to her. The aide had told me she was hard of hearing, and not to excite her because of her heart condition. Considering the purpose of my visit, I was afraid that might be a difficult assignment.

"Hello. I'm Ty Pierson," I said loudly.

A ray of comprehension lit up her features. "So you're the young man they told me was coming?"

"Yes ma'am. How are you feeling?"

"No need to shout. I hear you. They think I don't hear because I only listen when I feel like it."

I smiled. "Mrs. Bouchette ... "

"It's Ellie, young man. The Bouchettes can all go straight to hell. They put me in here, you know."

"What happened?" I asked, hoping the conversation would eventually go where I wanted.

"Bastards stuck me in here as soon as they got that power-of-attorney, I think they call it. Sold everything. Said I couldn't take care of myself. Got a doctor to agree with them. Damn the sorry bunch of them."

"What relatives do you have?"

"My sister-in-law and her brats, mostly. My Martha wasn't here to stop them. They cleaned my money out and acted like they were doing me a favor." Her features softened. "Listen to me, going on about my history. I'm sure you didn't come to hear about that, did you?"

"That's all right, Ellie. I'd like to hear about your daughter."

"Martha? She's a fine woman. Lives out on the coast, she and her daughter. She's my only grandchild, you know."

"I used to know your daughter. I wonder if there's some way to reach her?"

"Oh, she hasn't been here in years. She's much too busy. She's an actress, you know."

"I didn't know that." By now, I did know why Ellie was here, regardless of her age.

"Yes. And Jennifer too "

"Jennifer?"

"My granddaughter, just a little spit of a girl, but so full of life. Even though they can't visit, they talk to me quite often."

"That's nice that they call you."

"Heavens, no. I don't have a telephone. Don't need it. They tell me when to turn on my TV set so I can see them. Isn't that nice?"

"You see them on TV, do you?"

"Almost every night," she chirped.

No matter how splintered the windmills of Ellie's mind, I wanted to press on. Although I was entering dangerous waters now, I had to probe, knowing this was my best chance of getting some answers. "Ellie, I heard that Martha had an accident years ago … that she was hurt."

Mrs. Bouchette's cheerful demeanor clearly changed. She looked at me with suspicion. "Who told you that? Is that what those Bouchettes told you?"

"No. I just heard—"

"What was your name again?"

"Ty Pierson, ma'am."

She seemed to brighten a bit. "Oh, Ty Pierson. You're my Martha's friend. She talks about you all the time and so does Jennifer. All the time," she said beaming, showing her dentures. "But why are you here? You should be with her. She needs you."

I didn't know what to say. If I brought up Martha's *accident* again, it would probably set her off.

Making up my mind to pay a visit to the relative I had spoken to earlier, I tried to end my stay with Ellie in a pleasant way.

"I'm going to get in touch with her, Ellie. I'll sure do that."

"There's a good boy. Martha always tells me how she needs that Ty Pierson. That's what she says. My granddaughter is just a child, you know, and she needs a man's influence to keep her safe."

"Goodbye Ellie. It was nice talking to you."

The old woman's features turned dark. "My daughter's dead.

You killed her," she said flatly with eyes that had gone stone cold, as if she'd fallen into a trance. "Where were you when she needed you? *You killed her! You killed her! You murderer!*"

The charge nurse arrived, going to the old woman and patting her hand.

I rose and backed away, shocked at the change in her personality. Everyone I was meeting lately seemed to have a dark side.

"It's all right, Ellie. It's okay." Then, to me, the nurse said, "What did you say to her?"

"We were just talking about her daughter."

Ellie was quiet now and seemed unaware of my presence. The nurse led me into the hallway.

"If you know about her daughter, why come to ask a lot of questions?"

"I *don't* know about her. I just needed some information."

"As you can see, the woman is delusional. Shouldn't even be in a nursing home. We get quite a few that lose their grip on reality, and the money's not there for proper treatment. We don't need to have people coming around and dragging up the past. It doesn't help anyone, especially someone who's been through what this poor woman has."

"I understand," I said without trying to defend myself. "I'm sorry. I hope she gets better."

"They never get better," said the nurse. "They just get more and more out of touch. Then they die."

Without giving myself time to get discouraged, I headed straight to the nephew's house. He wouldn't care to dig into the past either, but I was more determined than ever to find out the circumstances of Martha's death. Ever since Michelle had been with me, ignorance had been bliss. For better or worse, I reckoned those times had ended.

***

I sat on another stakeout. Two hours passed before a car pulled into the driveway of a modest home in the Washington Park area, one of Denver's older neighborhoods. The red taillights flashed on and off, and then a man and a woman closed their car doors, climbed up the short flight of stairs and disappeared inside.

Giving them only a few minutes to think their day was winding down, I knocked. The burly man answered the door.

"Yeah? How can I help you?"

"I'm Ty Pierson. All I'm asking for is five minutes of your time for a few questions and I promise never to darken your door again."

He shrugged, figuring I wouldn't go away.

"Five minutes. No more."

Once inside, his wife peeked in and, deciding her presence wasn't needed, disappeared.

"What I need to know, Mr. Bouchette, is what happened when Martha left here and why did she kill herself? Whatever you can tell me will be of great comfort."

"Did you talk to my aunt Ellie?"

"Yes, I did."

"Well then, she must've told you Martha was alive and well and living it up."

"That's a sad situation. Maybe she's better off with her fantasies."

"Oh yeah. She's crazier than a shithouse rat, is what she is," he said with no sympathy in his voice. "Who're you? Some old boyfriend, or something?"

"An old friend."

"You think I can give you your answer in five minutes?" he asked. "We're all still trying to figure out what made Martha tick."

I just looked at him, expectantly.

He sighed heavily, knowing he was stuck with me. "What I know is, she got herself knocked up. She still lived with my aunt who was on the religious side. The guy wouldn't marry her, or couldn't marry her, or whatever, so her mom shipped her off to

Oregon. That's what they did with pregnant daughters back then, you know. Shipped them off somewhere. So, she gets out there, has her baby and then comes back."

"So she did come back and live in Denver?"

"For awhile. I guess she still had a thing for this stiff who knocked her up. When that didn't pan out, she took the kid and went back to Portland. She had some kind of deal in show business, supposedly."

"You don't know what she actually did?"

"Not for sure, but what I heard through the grapevine is that she was having a hard time making ends meet with the kid and all. My guess is she ended up taking off her clothes on stage or in bed, or both. She was a good looking broad when she was in her twenties, I'll give her that."

"And then what?"

"The 'then what' is, she suffocates her little girl and blows a major hole through her head, that's what. End of story."

"You don't know who the father of the girl was?"

"No, I don't and if you don't mind, you've had your five minutes. I've got things to do."

***

When I got home, Michelle's car sat in the drive. My plan shifted quickly, deciding to take Mama Shari's most recent advice. I wouldn't show all my cards. In the end, I showed none of my cards that night as Michelle presented me with a gift to put in the place where my ceramic stein had been. It was an expensive, sculpted marble torso resembling Michelle to the extent that she could have modeled for it. She didn't say a word about Boulder, or the three days since I had last seen her. All she said was that she wanted to make love to me, as I had never known love before. And she did, and in the process, chased away my demons, at least for a while.

CHAPTER 11

Once Michelle left again, I mentally perused the information before me. An old girl friend pulled a homicide/suicide. It was tragic, but what was my connection? Could Martha's daughter have been mine? If so, why wouldn't she have let me know? I played time-math trying to remember exactly when I was with Martha and then Carol. The news article had not revealed the age of the murdered child.

What about the other facts? Mama Shari had beamed up a name from my past that came to a tragic end. I'd gotten the idea that Michelle and Mallory Smith were sharing the same personality. Michelle was not what she seemed to be, either to me or to her father. Butch and Mama both warned me to be careful. And last but not least, the paranormal activity, which had become more and more aggressive, only took place in Michelle's absence.

The conclusions: There's a spirit world and someone in it is pissed off enough to turn my life topsy-turvy. Or, was there something in this bipolar Michelle reeking havoc? Yet Michelle had invigorated me, kept me on this side of the deep end. Maybe it was a trap, not only for me, but my son as well. What could I do to resolve it all?

When Michelle returned the next evening, I told her how much she walked, talked, laughed and acted like Mallory. Laughing, she credited my son with extremely good taste and thought my seeing her in other people meant she was on my mind. Her feminine wilds disengaged my fear once again.

There was a break in Michelle's graduate course schedule and she spent an entire weekend with me. I guess you could call it quality time. She even posed for me and my fears were diluted further when the photos turned out to be just as I had shot them.

Soon after our weekend, I decided to take some time and hit the open road, all by myself. I needed to get lost in the mountains for a few days with my camera to get a fresh perspective on things.

Ryan was staying busy with his new job and girl friend. Michelle was making her push toward her degree, spending time at the library and work, so the time was right.

I spoke to Butch before I left, thanked him for his continuing concern, and told him not to worry about little old me. Everything was under control, so I stayed away from the subject of my house and its guest. No need to drag anymore of my laundry past him. My hope had been that he wouldn't someday turn up with a cackling girlfriend.

"I think it would do you good to get out of Dodge for awhile," he agreed. "Give me a call as soon as you get back and we'll go see the Rockies get clobbered, my treat. And, I want to discuss something with you."

"What's it about?" I'd asked, but he said it was no big deal and could wait till I got back.

Curious as to how Michelle would receive my plans, I was surprised when she seemed to be all for my mini-vacation, saying she would use the time to get some serious studying done.

So the Jag and I set out for points west. I planned to hike a trail or two, enjoy a few mountain towns and meadows, and feel the sun on my face.

I avoided the phone the first couple of days, fighting the urge to call Michelle. I tried to think of little more than the natural beauty around me. From Ouray, my third night out, I did call, but if Michelle was there, she didn't answer. Then I called Ryan and left him a message. I guess I just wanted to know how he and Mallory were getting along, and wondered if I needed to express my misgivings. He would think I was crazy unless I told him about the tattoo. I would talk about it when I could speak to him live.

That evening, I walked the streets, puttered in the shops, and hit a restaurant/bar. But at bedtime, I pined for my mistress of the night. Sometimes I could almost hear her calling me, like Circe's sirens calling to Ulysses.

Two days later, I found myself in the San Luis Valley, walking the Great Sand Dunes. Going through a roll of film, I pictured Michelle naked, stretched out in the sand, like an Ed Weston photo. From the Alamosa Inn, I called again that evening, leaving a message this time, in case Michelle wanted to call.

In an hour, she did.

"Ty?" she said. "Something has happened."

"What?" It popped into my mind that my poltergeist had tired of waiting for me and had started without me, or that Mr. Devin had taken advantage of my absence and convinced Michelle to move out.

"It's your friend, Butch. There was a message when I came in."

"Michelle, what happened to Butch?"

"He's dead, Ty. It was his ex-wife that left the message."

"You're joking with me," I exclaimed, not believing.

"I wish I were."

This isn't happening, my mind screamed. "How?"

"That's all the message said. That he was dead. God, I feel so bad for you."

"I'm coming home. I'll talk to you when I get there."

I desperately tried Butch's number. No answer. About five hours, I calculated, and I could be home. I would call somebody then. I drove through the night, numbed by what I had been told, and tortured that I had no more information.

For once, Michelle was there, waiting up for me. She was subdued and willing to offer support if I wanted it, but content to be still and leave me alone with my thoughts. My mind still had not accepted the news even after the long, tiring drive. It was too much to bear, so I was somewhere in a void, beyond feeling or reacting.

✲✲✲

Unable to reach Doris the next day, I called one of my ex-coworkers. John and Butch were fairly close, not close like Butch and I, but he was someone who would make a point of finding out what he could.

"Butch was murdered. The police are calling it a botched drug deal, or a plain old-fashioned robbery."

"That's bullshit," I said, seething. "That's what they always say when they don't have a clue. Butch didn't have an enemy in the world that I know of."

"That's what I told Doris. She didn't believe it either," John said, trying to keep his voice from quivering. "Hell, as far as him having anything of value, Doris had already picked him pretty clean. She's in pretty bad shape, though. Her son losing his father and all."

"So the cops don't know what happened?"

"Who knows? There's an investigation. That's all they told Doris."

"What about Butch's funeral?" I asked.

"This Friday. Riverside."

***

The funeral was low-key. I had hoped for a spiritual choir. Thought Butch might have gotten a kick out of that, but Doris hadn't gone that route, just religious music via cassette over the PA system. I was still in shock by the suddenness of his passing. I had been prepared for Carol's death. Even though the cancer had moved through her body quickly, there had been time to evaluate. I didn't know when the impact of this most recent loss would hit me.

Most of Butch's coworkers were present, most of whom I knew. "Who would have thought we'd be meeting again this way?" one said, sitting next to me in the pew.

Butch's son, Joe, was a young man now. After the service, I told him what a great guy his dad had been, but I was pretty sure he already knew. As the smokers milled around in a group outside puffing on their cancer sticks, waiting for the casket to be brought out, I found John.

"Hey, Ty. How's retirement?"

"I've seen better days than today."

"Hell of a thing, isn't it?"

"Anymore information about what happened?"

"Not really. Nothing we'd know about anyway. It sure won't be the same around the water cooler without old Butchie, though."

"Mr. Pierson," someone called.

I turned around to see Mama Shari. Until that moment, I hadn't allowed myself to create any link between my problems and what had happened to Butch. I didn't want to give it that much credit.

Excusing myself, I left John to another drag on his coffin nail, and walked over to Mama.

"What a terribly sad day," Mama said. "You know, I never met Mr. Washington, but I felt I knew him from the few times we spoke. He was a true friend to you," she said. "True friendship is a rare and cherished thing."

"It hasn't really hit me yet," I told her, suddenly feeling like I might burst into tears and cry on her shoulder at any moment.

"That often happens. You've certainly had your share of grief."

I nodded.

"Will you walk with me for a minute?"

We strolled to the far end of the mortuary's freshly mowed lawn and I took the opportunity to apologize for not getting back to her about my research on Martha Bouchette.

"I need to hear about that too," she said, "but I want you to know that Butch called again about a week ago. He was pretty shook up the other time I talked to him, but this time it was more than that. He'd come to the conclusion that your houseguest was behind the paranormal activity, and thought I might be able to influence you into, shall we say, another arrangement. He was concerned about the relationship to the point that he went to where she worked."

I looked into Mama's eyes. "He never mentioned that. What did he tell you?"

"That Michelle isn't who you think she is."

I didn't tell her it wasn't the first time I'd been told that, or felt it myself.

"He went to the shop and asked for her. She assisted him and he left."

I waited.

"The girl who waited on him wasn't the girl he met at your house. He said there was a resemblance, but no amount of beauty aids could have transformed this girl into your Michelle. He said this girl had no memory of meeting him, and when he mentioned you, all he got was a blank stare."

"I wish he had talked to me."

"He was going to discuss it with you. I think he just wanted to run it past me first, maybe to make sure he wasn't losing his grip. That your situation wasn't rubbing off on him and into his head, and get my feelings as to what I might think was happening?"

"And what do you think now?"

"I think it's time to find out who your imposter is with no more postponements. Tell her the jig's up. It's time to fish or cut bait, Mr. Pierson. I don't know if what happened to Butch is related, but it may be time to contact the authorities and ask them to run a check on this Michelle."

"Will they do that? What can I tell them? That someone living in my house is pretending to be someone she isn't, and could have something to do with Butch's murder, and that I don't know who she really is?"

"I was thinking more about advising them to check the whereabouts of Michelle at the time of the murder. That might be a start."

The casket was being placed inside the cream-colored hearse and we walked back.

"I can be present when you confront Michelle if you want," Mama offered.

"Thanks for the information," I answered. "I'll let you know what I'm going to do and when."

"You need to get those cards we talked about on the table. Please let me help you when you are ready. I don't want you to be alone at such an emotional time, and you may need someone else there. It might be safer."

But I wouldn't be alone. I would be with Michelle.

CHAPTER 12

I smoothed my wrinkled sheets and tried to sleep, but thoughts of Michelle devil-danced in the dark. Sweat sprung from the skin on my neck and soaked into my pillow even though the night was cool. I stared into the darkness, which was palpable. At this hour of the night, a man could go mad, I thought.

It was always like this now when I waited for Michelle, wondering if she would come to me. I tried thinking of other things; a book I'd read, a movie I'd seen, but they were too remote. I'd done little in the past weeks but be with Michelle, or think about her. I buried my face in the soggy pillow and searched for sleep.

The phone rang at two a.m. I didn't much like to answer the phone anymore, but Caller ID read "BOULDER COMMUNITY HOSPITAL."

"Hello," I said.

"Mr. Pierson?"

"Yes?"

"This is Janice Thompson. I'm the night nurse supervisor. There's been an accident."

My heart froze.

"Your son and a Ms. Smith were in a one-car collision. Your son is alive, Mr. Pierson, but he's in critical condition."

"My God!"

"He's in the Intensive Care Unit. He suffered bruises and lacerations of his upper body. He also has a head injury."

I felt as if my emotions dropped out of me and landed on the floor. "Is he ... will he?"

"He's in a coma. You should probably get over here."

Adrenalin kicked in. "And the girl?"

"I'm afraid the woman was killed in the accident." She hesitated, choosing her words carefully. "I know you're terribly distraught, sir, but please drive carefully. We don't need to have you get in a wreck as well."

I was in the car and heading north within five minutes. Desolation swept over me, creating a world of emptiness. Why didn't I insist that Ryan quit seeing this girl the moment I knew there was something amiss? A thousand catastrophic images assaulted me. Every horrible vision of an accident scene my mind could concoct reared its ugly head as I drove recklessly through the night to be with my son.

At the hospital, I approached the check-in counter fearing the worst. A doctor corralled me before I went tearing through the place.

"Ryan is a very lucky young man. The force of the accident killed Mallory Smith instantly, but Ryan was wearing his seat belt, keeping him in the vehicle. His contusions are not serious, but he's still in a coma, and with a head injury you just never know."

The idea of seeing Ryan in a hospital bed hooked to monitors and fastened to tubes ... like Carol ... terrified me. "When can I see him?" I asked.

"Give us a little more time and we'll let you in. Remember though, he won't be responsive yet." Knowing I needed more than that, he patted my arm and added, "He's young and strong. With a little luck, he'll pull out of this."

"All right, Doctor. Just let me know when I can see him."

A police officer waited until the doctor sauntered down the hall before approaching me. It was all starting to settle in now. I was on the verge of breaking down. Dealing with this cop temporarily delayed the overload.

"Mr. Pierson? I'm sorry to trouble you now, but maybe we can complete our investigation if you'll give me a few minutes?"

"What investigation?" I said wearily.

"Just routine. Was the girl driving a close friend of your son's?"

"They've been seeing each other for a few months."

"The relationship was going well as far as you know?"

"I have no reason to think differently."

"The reason I ask, sir, is apparently there was no attempt on the young lady's part to stop the vehicle."

"You mean she crashed on purpose?" I said, not sure anything would truly surprise me any longer.

"It appears that way. No skid marks. It looks like she ran directly into the largest barricade she could find. Can you give me any information about her at all?"

"I just met her once. She just graduated, looking for a job. That's about it."

"Thank you," he said, willing to leave me with my thoughts. "I hope your son pulls through okay. A crash like this is most always fatal if people don't wear seat belts. Be thankful your son did."

I nodded and tried to smile.

"One last question. From a preliminary examination, it appears this girl was pregnant. Do you have any idea if your son was aware of this?"

"No. No idea," I answered, bewildered. "I didn't know either."

They let me sit in Ryan's room for the night. He made no

sounds or movement. Only the maddening rhythm of the respirator breathing for him and the beep-beep of the EKG monitor interrupted the silence. If I lost him, I really didn't know if I could go on. What a dreary place the world would be without him, I thought. I felt responsible. Something I had done, or didn't do had led to this. If I was right about whatever was in Michelle being in Ryan's girlfriend, then it was my fault. I had opened the door somehow.

As I sat with my head in my hands, the sun peeking through the window blinds, I heard something. Someone calling my name. I thought I must have been dozing. Then, I heard it again.

"Dad?"

I looked up and Ryan had turned his head in my direction. Leaping from the chair, I went to his bedside and took his hand. "Ryan?"

"Dad," he said again, faintly.

He closed his eyes and turned his face toward the ceiling. I thought he was unconscious again, but then he said, "Seat belt. She ... so fast."

"What is it, son?"

"Seat ... She tried to unhook my seatbelt. She tried ... why would she?"

I ran down the hall to grab the first nurse I could find.

CHAPTER 13

Darkness had seeped into my soul. It blanketed the rooms of my house like the inside of a tomb. I sensed unseen movement. Something in the dark tried to speak to me, but nothing affected me now. I no longer worried about moving objects. I'd stopped keeping house long ago. Dust coated my personal treasures like snow on a dead animal. I felt like a bear cub inside his den. I hesitated leaving for fear I might lose my way back to safety ... to the place where Michelle surrounded me. I had been feeling both sane and crazy, trying to accept the reality of something I had always believed impossible. Was my mind coming apart at the seams? I didn't think so … not any longer. Things had gone beyond my fear of insanity.

As I slouched on the sofa, ensconced against one of its arms, I waited alone in the dark, my eyes riveted on the front door. Although I was the sole human inhabitant at the moment, I sensed Michelle's immediate presence. She was in the sofa's throw pillows she had hugged to her breasts the first night. She was in the dregs of the wineglass I couldn't bring myself to wash. The smell of her body was in the sheets where we had laughed and made love. Physical traces were everywhere, but what about her soul? Was there a dark place in her that crawled with destruction and deceit? Was I nothing more than a senile old fool? I had to know once and for all who Michelle was, and why she had come into my life.

My friend had been taken from me and very nearly, my son. I was isolated now and my time was at hand. All my ills pointed to my housemate. If she wanted to destroy me, she could have slit my throat dozens of times while I lay sleeping. The truth would never be known unless Michelle talked.

I had waited for three nights. She always returned by the third night. I felt old and brittle as if I had aged years since meeting Michelle. My features sagged under the weight of what I planned to do. This time I had a gun, and if need be, I'd use it.

Then I heard her car pull in the drive. I heard her footsteps on the porch and the key slip into the lock. The door opened. There she stood, silhouetted in the moonlight, much the way I'd seen her the first night when she changed my life. She was the prettiest creature I had ever seen.

I was torn between love and hate, in no-man's land. "Leave it open. You may not want to stay."

"Why are you sitting in the dark?"

"Why do you disappear for three days whenever something happens to someone I care about?"

She came to me. Her hand reached out to my face. I pulled away. She sat next to me on the couch.

"Ty, you know you're safe with me."

"Safe? Your kind of safety could kill a man."

"Death is nothing to fear," she said soothingly. "Especially when it comes in the presence of someone you love. There are forces greater than you know. Forces I don't understand myself. I am here to help you this one last time.

"I don't believe any of this. Forces from where?"

"From the other side of life."

I moved to where she could see my weapon, but I was unable to point it at her. "Just explain it to me, would you? Why am I losing everyone?"

"But I'm here with you and this is your destiny, to be with the ones who have always needed you."

She moved closer, unimpressed with the pistol. I let her stroke my brow. Her fingers were cool against my skin. A hint of perfume. Everything about her had become familiar. I felt her breath on my neck. Her breathing was the only sound in the room.

"Who or what are you?" I asked.

"You want to know the truth? The truth often maims and kills, doesn't it? Poor, innocent Ty." Her emerald eyes seemed to look through me. "Then, I will tell you a story."

"I'm listening," I said resolutely, determined not to let her charm take hold of me as it had always done.

She spoke softly, almost hypnotically. "A woman bore your child. A child you were never permitted to know. Your wife wasn't about to let another woman take you away. The bitch offered money for the woman to disappear. When that didn't work, your wife hired a man to assault the woman. But the woman kept trying to reach you."

I looked at Michelle, shaking my head slightly, saying nothing.

Michelle smiled. "That's right. Your darling Carol kept the ones who needed you most away from you."

"You're saying Martha Bouchette had my child? Surely no one could have kept her from reaching me some way? A telephone call?"

"Your wife had powers of which you weren't aware. She knew you would choose the woman who'd carried your firstborn. Her desire to keep you was so strong that she sacrificed a child for a child."

"What?"

"Your precious Carol sacrificed the woman's child and had your son, Ryan. He should never have been born."

The story was too bizarre and unreal. I had no idea of this woman's obsession. I didn't want to hear anymore of this nonsense and started to move away.

Michelle grabbed my wrist. Her green eyes narrowed, her mouth had a scornful twist. She looked beautiful and terrible at the same time. "You want to know who I am. Let me finish my story. On earth, your wife's power was too strong, but in death, it was equalized. After that, my mother waited for the opportunity to reach you. Through the living you see, she could again experience the pleasures of the flesh."

"But how could Carol have sacrificed anyone. Martha killed herself and her child?"

"You still don't understand, my darling," Michelle cooed, her stare mesmerizing. "She didn't kill herself. Your wife killed her along with her daughter."

She paused for effect. I stared, hypnotized by her story and overpowering presence. Her strength was greater than mine.

"Carol used to take those business trips, sometimes to Portland, in case you don't remember. There was no reasoning with a woman so determined to keep her little world intact. But even she couldn't kill the cancer when it came to take her, could she?"

"This can't be true. How could you possibly know any of this?"

"Oh, but I would know if I were there. If I were the woman's daughter."

I was looking into the eyes of an impossibility. An irresistible urge forced me to study Michelle more closely. I remembered the thread of familiarity I'd felt the day I saw her at the ice cream shop. Suddenly everything seemed believable.

"If Carol had not put a gun to my mother's head and the pillow over my face," she said wistfully, as if she was remembering the scene. "If I had been allowed to live, you would've known a beautiful, intelligent daughter. I could've had my own wonderful life with a mother and father. But your wife wouldn't allow that. Instead, I've learned about love and lust through this pathetic host. With mother's help, we created what I would have become. She and I together have, at least, known your human form for awhile."

"Jennifer."

"How gratifying that you finally know my name."

Her hands moved toward my lap. I'd forgotten about the gun. She picked up the pistol and admired it as if it was a delicate piece of china, turning it in her hands.

"You're right," she said. "The time has come for the truth. No more pretending. You must take the final step and come with me now." She placed the weapon in my hand and closed her hands around mine. "Don't worry, lover. This isn't the end of a movie where the killer tells all to the victim, and someone is murdered. There's been enough murder. No, Ty, your blood won't be on our hands. You need to do this yourself. You want to. It'll be like a wedding night. Mother and I want to be with you for eternity. We've lost so much time. You wouldn't want to be with Carol after what you've discovered?"

My chest tightened with fear, but I was at the same time titillated by her touch. Captivated by the sound of her voice, I sat there thinking nothing, waiting.

"And you've gotten a gun." Her voice still held a smile. "You must have been planning it already?"

"I was planning to use it on you, for what you did to Ryan."

"Shhh," she whispered, putting her finger on my lips, marrying her soul to mine for eternity. "You could never kill the image of your own flesh and blood."

My willpower was compromised. I was near shock at her revelations. Part of my mind remained horrified by what this being who called herself 'Jennifer' was asking me to do. But another part thought about the pain I'd caused for the woman that bore my first child. I could feel the savage texture of it through Michelle's words. It flooded over me and made me yearn for sleep, and perhaps, even death.

"It's so easy. My mom and I were murdered because of our desire to be with you. You need to do this for us." She turned my hand with hers to where the muzzle pointed at my temple. She smiled again. It was a cold, secret smile. "Just squeeze, Daddy. Squeeze the trigger and we'll all be together."

I closed my eyes, not wanting to see Michelle's calm, beautiful face asking me to take my life.

"So easy, so quick. Don't you want to be with us?" she asked.

Death whispered in my ear telling me to let go of life. My resistance faded. I didn't want to disappoint the creature next to me even though I knew she was gone forever. I wanted my world to go back to the once-upon-a-time of our first encounter. Maybe my death was for the best. I decided to do it.

"Pierson " someone yelled.

Opening my eyes, I saw Michelle's father in the doorway. Moving quickly, his hands were on the weapon, joining ours.

"No " Michelle screamed.

My hand came free as they fought for control of the gun. As I watched them struggle, everything seemed to move in slow motion. Even though Devin had a hundred pound advantage, the young woman hung on to the weapon as they wrestled around the room. They looked like two novice tango dancers trying frantically to learn their steps. Suddenly, with a burst of strength, Michelle tore free with the gun still in her hands. Devin backed away from her and literally sat on my lap, protecting me.

"Michelle, listen," he said. "Come out of this now It's not you wanting to do this. Whoever you are inside Michelle, whatever happened to you, it's not my daughter's fault. You've got to let her go and you've got to let this man live. Let her go."

"All we want is to be together, Jennifer said. We're trying to save him, not harm him. This hasn't been easy. We need him now." She pointed the gun at the two of us.

"You'll have him in due time," Devin said, trying to calm the spirit within Michelle, "but not till his time comes. Not this way."

"Mother won't wait. Don't you understand? It's got to be now."

"Michelle," Devin pleaded. "If you're there, I know you can't kill."

She seemed to be wavering. Devin got off me and slowly approached her, holding out his hand for the gun.

Suddenly Michelle cackled. Her demeanor changed. "If Jennifer can't do it, I can."

Mother had taken over.

Devin lunged for the gun and Michelle shot him in the shoulder. He fell to his knees, grimacing, holding his wound.

"Now look what you've made me do." Now Michelle's voice was filled with fury.

"Martha," I said. "I'm so sorry for what happened, but I'm not going. You don't want more victims. If you love me so much, stop this."

"Please take your life now," Martha pleaded through Michelle, who no longer looked beautiful, only desperate. "I can't take it for you. We'll leave together."

I sensed another presence. For just a moment—an instant—I

saw the shape of a woman silhouetted in the open door Devin had entered. "Carol?" my tongue tried to say, but couldn't.

"*Leave herrrr!*" the electronic voice screamed as the marble torso sailed across the room, striking Michelle with a glancing blow. Michelle's scalp started to bleed.

"I'm still having to fight for you even now," Martha cried sorrowfully.

"I won't do it, Martha. I won't go. You can't force me. I want you to let go of Michelle."

She hesitated for what seemed an eternity and then lowered the gun in frustration and resignation. "Then, I'll have to fight for you another time. If only humans could understand. You're a blind man, but eventually you'll see." Almost as an afterthought, she smiled sadly and said, "Just so you don't forget us again." Michelle placed the gun barrel in her mouth and pulled the trigger.

Even before I could scream "NO" the act was done. I watched in horror as the flash lit the inside of Michelle's head and the sound of the weapon echoed through my house. Michelle's lifeless body fell to the floor near her father.

Breaking into sobs, Devin crawled next to his daughter, taking her hand. "How could she have done that? She couldn't kill you, but she could kill Michelle?" he said crying, ignoring his own wound.

"God help us, I don't know," was my meager reply, appalled at the action Jennifer and Martha had chosen to take.

Calling 911, I tried to comfort the man until help arrived. Though I didn't want to look, I was drawn to Michelle's face. The eyes no longer sparkled emerald. They were a dull brown. It wasn't the face of the Michelle I'd known. It was a stranger that lay dead on the floor. In spite of her violent demise there was a macabre serenity about her. She looked untroubled, yet sad, as if she knew she'd never be allowed to live out her life.

The Michelle I knew, the one who had given me the marble torso that now lay broken in the wreckage, the one that would have been my daughter if she had lived, was gone forever.

No longer was there a Martha or Jennifer to pull Michelle's strings. She had been an innocent pawn sacrificed to darker forces than even Mama Shari could ever have imagined, for lust and revenge from beyond the grave.

I had survived but at the terrible price paid by my son and two young girls, and Butch. And there was that buried secret of the woman with whom I'd shared twenty-five years of my life. What would become of her spirit? Could she ever be at peace if she had done what Jennifer claimed? Would the battle rage on at another time in another place?

CHAPTER 14

Thanks to Kenneth Devin's timely decision to end the relationship between Michelle and me, I am still around to speculate about those four months of my life. I'll never be able to completely understand or explain what took place, but I can try.

As Mama Shari and I have worked it out, Carol had the dark secret of thwarting Martha's attempts to reach me, aborting any continuance of a relationship between Martha and myself. Did she actually kill the woman and her daughter? We only have Jennifer's words.

Whether or not Carol was able to fool Portland authorities into believing a homicide was a suicide is open to debate. For the sake of argument, I'll say Jennifer was telling the truth.

So, here are mother and daughter, prematurely in the spirit world with unresolved issues about never being given the opportunity to have the life mother desired. As long as Carol was alive, she had some sort of power to keep away the spirits. But when she died, the major barrier was removed and an attempt to reunite with me could begin.

The other factor was that my state-of-mind had to be right. I had to be receptive to these spirits and as time went on, my unconscious became susceptible to Martha and Jennifer's wishes. Though they were spirits, Martha wanted to re-experience me physically, having been cheated in life, before taking me to the land beyond.

How wonderful and terrible life can be and I guess the same goes for death. Carol was not having the greatest of afterlives. First, she went to her grave, and then she could not rest for fear that Martha and Jennifer would win me over and cost me, and possibly Ryan, our lives. Carol's powers may have been diminished in death, but enough spiritual energy remained to try and warn me of the danger Martha and Jennifer presented.

How these beings could have existed in the real and the unreal world at the same time is a subject of conjecture, but Mama believes Jennifer and Martha's spirits were often at strategic war, hence Michelle's occasional conversations with herself. Jennifer beguiled me with a specter of herself, the girl she would have become, through someone similar in appearance. The host, an innocent Michelle, continued her life as normally as they would permit.

The same thing happened with Mallory. Jennifer and Martha, we presume, were occasional visitors inside Mallory, long enough to get Ryan's attention and try to kill him. Getting me was not enough in Martha's opinion. My son should never have existed. Taking him was part of some grand vendetta—a penance that had to be paid by working their magic on him through another individual who also resembled my daughter.

Michelle had been more than a phantom. She was flesh and blood. But the personality I knew was the result of spirits that had dwelt within her, spirits powerful enough to take on my daughter's appearance.

In the end, I try not to cast blame, considering the struggle was about being wanted, even in this bizarre way. That is what I have to keep telling myself. The good news is that Ryan is making progress. I know he'll never look at life in quite the same way. His invulnerability has been taken from him. But his life is something to be thankful for, and I'm not completely alone.

I have blood on my hands for the lives of my friend and two innocent girls to answer for. Martha and Jennifer did accomplish that, whispering their words of love and desire in my ear. They saw to it that I too, would learn about loss in a deeper way than I thought possible. Sometimes, I think it would have been better to let them take me.

The dead cannot visit the world by inhabiting the living, my handlers tell me, but I know differently unless, of course, I had spent a good part of the year in some state of mental deterioration. Could I be lost in my dementia? "Dementia praecox," I heard someone whisper. "A schizophrenic episode."

Where does awareness leave off and madness begin? To accept that I am mad is a tough concept for a rational person to swallow. The thing Mama had said about insanity being on a continuum we're all on to a greater or lesser degree comes to mind. Maybe it's just about that? Maybe I've been insane to the greater degree and living an illusion since the first time objects began to move? Maybe everything since then has been imagination?

That's what the so-called experts are telling me. Just conjecture. They say I'll have to face the fact that most everything was merely hallucination. They are studying my head, trying to figure me out. They don't put much stock in Mr. Devin or Mama's accounts of things. I may not be insane by any textbook definition, but I am most certainly haunted.

Presently, I'm happy with my son's rehabilitation, although I sometimes get a creepy feeling that Carol will walk in through the door the way she did the night she began moving things. The way she did when she saved my life.

All that's left of Michelle are the photos. Though they cause sadness, I look at them now and then. And I still dream of her ... the way she was when we first met. I wonder if I can ever lie down again without thinking about her legs intertwined with mine and hearing a redundant melody of my life's desire.

And on still, quiet evenings such as this one, I hear Michelle's voice like a gentle wave upon the shore, the sound of Jennifer's words in Michelle's mouth whispering in my ear ... calling ... calling.

Printed in the United States
82538LV00003B/263